Mystery
of the
Khar Chuluu

WILSON WHITLOW

For My Family

Cover illustration by Luciana Guerra

Mystery
of the
Khar Chuluu

Prologue

H ere is a book to be read out loud.

Does that surprise you?

Time was when all books were read that way. These marks on the page were nothing more than grooves for the mouth to follow. Monks in their cells could be heard day and night mumbling over their books.

Earlier still, the scribe read the scrolls to the Pharaoh. The Roman shouted his bills in the forum. The angels told the prophets, "Set this down," and their words were later spoken.

How do I know? I am the Djinn of All Deserts, who piles himself like a pillar of smoke and rolls across the ages. I doze away centuries. I fritter decades on a crossword puzzle. And I have seen many things. Many things.

I have seen the things I am about to tell you—or most of them. Some were hidden from my sight by the new science, some by the old science. But I know of what I speak. What I did not myself see has come to me by the most trustworthy of sources, as you yourself will soon see.

This story begins with a robbery and ends with a rescue. But that is not how I will tell it. For, as the poets and prophets have told me, it is best to keep some good bits in reserve.

Oh, and if you have heard my name you may have heard of my reputation. Cunning, I have been called. A liar, a trickster, and nothing more than a magical mercenary. All this and more is true—or once was. Slavery, it seems, brings out the worst in man, beast, and spirit.

But now. Now, I stand before you a free spirit, mighty in magic but humble by decision, a tongue of flame dancing perchance just outside your vision.

Chapter 1

*In which Chul Sun and Anita
Aminou beat each other silly just prior
to a very narrow escape from the
hands of Thorium Dare.*

The Two-Hearted Forest that night was a slurry of wind and tangled trees. A great bowl of darkness choked with blizzarding snow. Every warm-blooded thing curled in nooks or cowered under copses waiting out the night. Every warm-blooded thing, that is, but for a lonely figure stumbling against the wind that split to daggers through the trees and slashed his cheeks and stabbed him through his insufficient jacket.

Chul Sun was this person's name. A boy of ten

years, lost in the whirling darkness, he stumbled in his sneakers through the drifts that piled to his knees, his feet and fingers throbbing. But even though Chul Sun was tired and frozen to the marrow, he did the only thing he knew how to do: he soldiered on.

After some time, Chul blinked through the snow caking his eyelashes and saw something up ahead. A glint. A flicker of light. He had seen this, or something like it, many times that night and his first thought was to ignore it. It was only a mirage, a trick his eyes played in their desperate struggle to find some footing in the inky darkness all around him. But this time, there was something different. As he drew closer, it became a square, interrupted now and then by a branch or a tree trunk. It was there, all right, this light, though still at some distance from him. He quickened his pace, and saw, with a skip of his heart, that this was the outline of a window. Closer still, he could make out the panes, separated by the cross of the muntins, and after that, the edges of curtains, a potted flower on the sill, and, beyond, the butterscotch glow of a fire.

Soon, his face was hovering just inches from the glass, his breath frosting the pane. Inside, he saw a girl in silhouette seated in a cane-backed rocker. She had a mop of coily black hair tied loosely in a ponytail, a long neck, rich brown skin, eyes with dark lashes focused on a book she was holding in her lap. She was older than him, he could tell, but only by a year or two, and looking around the room in which she was seated, he was surprised to find that she was all alone.

His own cold disappeared out of concern for this girl in a cabin in the Two-Hearted Forest, even though his lot was far worse than hers. She was inside and warm and he was outside and frozen. Yet his only thought was to help her, somehow, in whatever way he could.

Just as that thought struck Chul, the girl turned toward the window with such intensity that he barely had time to duck. Fortunately, the boy moved faster than other people. Much faster. He moved so fast that he could evade notice or capture at will. He was, he was told, the fastest person on the planet.

He used this skill to sneak around the rough-hewn cabin to the front door, thinking that it would be better to knock than to spy any longer. He paused only a moment, remembering the black stone he was carrying inside the front pocket of his jeans. He could feel its energy, dark and tantalizing. Was it better to keep running, he wondered, than to stop here and linger, but the sting of cold was too much to endure a moment longer. He knocked. The sound was lost in the howl of the wind and snow. He reached out again just as the door swung open. The girl stood before him, one hand clutching the neck of a quilted robe under her chin.

"Who are you?" she said, her voice blunt with suspicion. She glanced warily over his shoulder. Chul was uncertain what she might be looking for out in the dark forest behind him.

"I was lost."

"You were lost?"

"I *am* lost. I saw the light in your window." The warmth of the cabin, the cozy fire called to him. "Are you all alone out here?"

"My parents went out," she replied. "I'm waiting for them." Again, she looked out into the darkness. "It's dangerous in the forest, especially at night. Where did you come from?"

"North."

"North? There's a lot of that from where we are."

"Look, it's a long story. It's really cold out here. Can you please let me in?"

At this, the girl drew her gaze together and looked into Chul's eyes. Hers were dark and penetrating, fierce and vulnerable at the same time. They seemed to be asking, *Can I trust you?*

He tried to reply with his own: *Yes, yes. Now let me in!*

She stepped aside. "Hurry up then."

He entered and she pressed the door shut against the wind. With a swish at the threshold, the howling died to a murmur. She locked, latched, and bolted the door. And, as if this were not enough, she then swung a thick hickory board across from jamb to jamb so that it could not open.

"Where are your parents?" Chul asked again.

"Out. They'll be back soon." She turned and watched him as he stamped and shivered off the cold. Clumps of snow fell on the floorboards.

"My name is Chul. Chul Sun."

"Anita is my name." She hesitated. "Anita Aminou. You can take your coat off and sit by the fire. Are you hungry?"

"I am, actually."

She went to a sideboard where there was a loaf

of bread and a small plate with softened butter. He had never spent time with other children, let alone girls, and he found her intensely interesting. She had a wide and gently upturned nose and smooth cheeks softly burnished in the fire light. She cut and buttered the bread with the same furrowed concentration as she had in admitting him to the cabin, and handed him the slices. Food in hand, he forgot about his interest in Anita, his coat, even the chill that still stiffened his hands. He devoured the bread. She cut three more slices and gave him warm buttermilk from the stove, which he drank down so fast that he burped despite himself.

"That's right," she said. "Daddy says burping's good for digestion." She smiled for the first time and took the cup from his hands. "You should sit. Give me your coat."

Chul pulled it off and sat down on a stool near the hearth. He looked around the cabin. It was a single room with a loft above, and, though small, it seemed ample due to its tidiness and the simplicity of its furnishings. He felt good here, and, though his company was just a young girl in a quilted robe, for the first time in a long time, he felt safe.

Anita sat down on the rocking chair where she had been reading. "Momma says you should never let strangers in at night. But my Gram says, in the old days, you *had* to let a stranger in. Would have been wrong to say no."

"What if the stranger was a thief?" asked Chul. "Or worse?"

"That's why you have to ask them, in the eyes, if they are kind or no."

"I felt you asking me."

"And I felt you answering. So I let you in. Gram says there has to be some trust in this dark world and wide."

"When will your parents come back?" he asked again. He felt for the stone in his pocket, thinking he should probably move on before they returned. He did not know what the stone was, but knew that he could not be caught with it.

"Soon enough, I expect," she said, but then stood up suddenly, her body rigid with attention.

Chul stood too, his body stiffened for fight or flight. "What—" She shushed him with a gesture. Her whole body seemed to be listening. All he could hear was the muted howl of the storm and the crackle of the fire. He watched as she went to the window, pulled the curtains tight, and came back to the center of the room. She closed her eyes, held her arms out to her sides, and with hands cupped loosely, turned in a circle. She looked to Chul like a radar antenna trained on the darkness beyond the cabin walls. When she turned full round, she opened her eyes and regarded him.

"What happened?" he asked. "What were you doing?"

"There's someone out there."

"Your parents?"

"No, not them. Someone else. And he is moving with purpose. You said you came down from the north?" Chul nodded. "This person is coming the same way. Down the bowl from the north."

Chul grabbed his coat. "I have to go."

Anita blocked his way to the door. "Do you know this person?"

"I do. And it's no one you want to meet."

"You can't go back into the snow and cold. Out there, you're in danger. In here, I will protect you."

"You'll protect me?"

She tensed at the question. "Yeah. Why not?"

"Well, no offense, but you're just a kid."

"*You're* a kid," she replied simply.

"Yes," he said, "but I have ways of escaping from people. I escaped from that man once, I can escape again."

"You can't escape from the night and the cold. What if you get lost?"

"I'll take my chances. Now, please let me go before I put you in danger too. Besides, if your parents come back there will be too much to explain. I can't have them taking me into town as a lost child. It will be worse if the police find out about me."

She had not moved from her position between him and the door. "I'm not letting you go."

He was impressed by her stubbornness and touched by her desire to protect him, but he could not see how she could possibly help, even if she did seem to have keen senses. "Let me go."

"Nope."

He saw that it was useless trying to talk this through. His only way out was to slip free. He figured that in less than half a second, he could go around her, dislodge the hickory crossbar from the door, unbolt, unlatch, and unlock it, and escape without breaking anything. He would have to get her off balance. He would feint to the left at normal speed and then charge right at super speed. She would never be able to lay a finger on him.

"Maybe you're right..." he said and lunged left. She stepped in front of him. He kicked into super speed, dodged right, then bolted for the door, but just as he did, something very unusual happened. He felt two skinny arms grab him from behind and lock him into a bear hug.

"Oh no you don't!" cried Anita.

Chul tried to slip out by dropping to his knees, but she was right with him. She followed his every move. "You're fast," she said, "but I can read you like a book. How was it that I saw you at the window, staring at me? Fact is, I could feel you coming for quite a while. You were walking zigzags out there in the snow like a lost calf. You go back out, you'll be doing the same. And that man coming down into the bowl will be on you like a duck on a June bug, you hear?"

He wriggled. Her grip tightened like finger locks. He considered his options. "Look," he said, "I don't know how you were able to catch me like that, and I admit, it's impressive, but you don't know what you're dealing with here. If you don't let me go, there's going to be big trouble for you and your parents."

"My parents can take care of themselves."

By the force of this girl's grip, Chul guessed they could.

"Let me go."

"No."

"OK," he said, "I didn't want to have to do this. And it's going to hurt. But it's only because you won't let me go."

"Do your worst," she said, cinching tighter.

"That's something you definitely *do not* want." With that, he blinked twice hard and felt his body rising on an updraft of electrons, dragging Anita up with it. Once airborne, he did the thing he hated to do: Blinking again, he released his grip on his inner regulator. He felt his atoms shiver on the cusp of an electromagnetic pulse that blew outward like the shockwave of a grenade. The force blew his jacket out of his hand and the shoes off of his feet; books were thrown from shelves; the bread and butter toppled from the sideboard. She fell with a shriek onto her back. Chul took one regretful glance at the senseless girl on the floor. She would wake up in a few minutes. He wanted to clean up the mess he had made, but there was no time. If Thorium Dare truly was on his way, he had to leave now or he would surely put this girl in danger.

He grabbed his shoes and jacket and flipped up the crossbar blocking the door. But as soon as he did, it slammed down, nearly lopping off his fingers. He turned around fast and found her on her feet, her quilted robe blown back so he could see her floral flannel pajamas, chestnut toes set on the floorboards ready for a fight. "I said, you're not going out there again!"

"Oh yes I am!" growled Chul. He put out an open hand and sent an electrical pulse at her. Anita stepped easily out of the way and the pulse dashed a row of porcelain figurines from the mantel. He threw another pulse, which again she dodged. A storm lamp shattered. "This is useless," he muttered and, eying the window to his right, decided to smash his way out. He balled up his jacket on his fist and leaped toward the window. But instead of hitting the glass, he rebounded off the side of the rocking chair that she had whisked in front of the window without even touching it.

Chul fell backwards and lunged straight for the stubborn girl. The next moment, they were locked in dire battle. Dishes shattered. Walls shuddered. Pillows exploded into clouds of feathers. The rocking chair splintered to pieces. He parried left and right at fantastic speed and shot bolts of energy at her. Anita seemed to anticipate his every move and was always somewhere else entirely: behind him, to the right, to the left, up in the loft and sending a cascade of objects down upon him: books, toothbrushes, andirons, boots. He was forced to flee in circles below her, under a bubble of bluish energy, the household objects bouncing off without effect. He tried to get close to the door or to the window, but the girl had piled mattresses and the sideboard in the way. The bread and butter were slicked in a mess on the floor.

"Your mom and dad sure are going to be mad, Anita!"

"Don't worry about me," she said. "I always clean up my messes!"

She sent a rope after Chul and caught him by the foot. The rope coiled like a vine around his ankle. He cut it with a bolt of energy. It leaped after him again. While he was distracted by the rope, she jumped at him and wrapped her vise-like grip around him. "Do you give up?"

"Of course not." And then: "Sheesh, you're

squeezing my guts out!"

Her body tensed in concentration, her arms still locked around Chul.

"I think I just pooped!" he said.

"Shush!" she hissed. With her arms still around him, she closed her eyes and doused the lanterns. The cabin was plunged into darkness.

"What—"

"Quiet! Listen."

Chul listened. All he could hear was the whirl and whistle of the wind outside, the sound of branches clattering against each other. But then he heard what she heard: Something or someone was stomping around the outside of the cabin, making a dull thumping on the walls. He knew at once that this was the person who had followed him down into the bowl and had, no doubt, tracked his footprints to this very spot. Now he truly *had* put Anita in grave danger.

The person stopped outside the door and pounded once, twice. "Chul? Dude, are you in there?"

"Who's that?" whispered Anita.

"His name is Thorium Dare."

"Chul?" came the man's voice again. "Come out, little buddy. Let's go back. We'll eat some pizza, play some Super Smash Bros. Just buds chillin' in the hacienda. Whaddaya say?"

"That's Thorium Dare? Are you sure?" asked Anita.

"Of course. Why? How do you know him?"

"Everybody knows about the Dares. His great-granddad was like super famous — but in a bad way. It's just that I didn't expect *him* to sound so — I don't know — dumb."

"He isn't as dumb as he sounds. I should know. Look, you have to let me get out of here. Go up into the loft and hide. He may think I'm alone."

She loosened her grip. "No. There is another way. Follow me."

She guided him along the ground to the center of the room where she pulled back the carpet. He could not see what she was doing but could hear her groping along the floorboards.

"Chul? I'm getting annoyed out here," shouted Dare. "This cold's freezing my sinuses. It's like someone's stabbed me between the eyes with an ice pick. Come out now, and let's get out of here."

Anita seemed to have found what she was looking for. Chul heard the brush and click of metal. She slapped his foot and whispered, "Start talking. Make some noise."

"What do you want me to say?"

"Anything, stupid. Just start talking…"

"Who's in there with you? Are you making new friends?"

"No, no!" Chul yelled. He stood up and stomped around. "I'm just finding my shoes!"

"You're a pretty crummy liar, bud. That's something we're going to have to work on. God! My head is killing me. Dude, open this door before my frickin' brain freezes!"

Anita hoisted something off the floor and Chul smelled an updrafting odor of cold soil. A trap door! He heard her scramble down in. He scurried toward her.

"Yes! Yes!" he yelled. "You're right. We will have to work on my lying. OK. Found my shoes! I'll be right out!"

"*Liar*!" There was a blast like a shotgun, and the door leaped off its hinges. Another blast and the wooden crossbar snapped. Anita grabbed him with her vise-like grip and pulled him down into the passage under the cabin. She shut the hatch above them.

"You didn't tell me there was a trap door!"

"I was too busy kicking your butt…"

"You didn't kick my butt. I kicked *your* butt!"

"Chul?" yelled the man above them, now inside the cabin. "Where did you go now?"

"Uh, yeah," said Anita, "hold that thought. We better get out of here. Follow me." She grabbed the scruff of his shirt and pulled him roughly along the passage.

Chapter 2

*In which Anita Aminou and Chul
Sun give Thorium Dare the slip and
end up talking to a tree.*

Chul followed Anita along the cramped passage that burrowed under and away from cabin. He elbowed on dirt, squiggled, scrambled, and crawled until, with a shift of soil, he felt her disappear in front of him. Moving forward, he felt the bottom of the passage open and, reaching down, found he could not touch the bottom of the hole. This fresh dark, strangely, was darker, more complete, than the mere pitch black of the passage.

"Where did you go?" he whispered.

"Just go into the hole," came her reply, which,

even more oddly, sounded as if it were coming from right in front of him instead of from below.

"I can't touch bottom."

"There is none. Just come through. It's hard for me to keep this open and your friend will be following us any second now."

Sure enough, Chul's "friend" had discovered the trap door and he could hear, behind and above him, the hatch being thrown open.

"Chul!" called Dare. "What are you doing down there? Look, I swear if you don't come back up here I'm going to kick the living stuffing out of you. Do you want that? You insanely annoying brat! And don't think I'm climbing down there after you! Oh no, dude, you're coming back to *me*!"

The soil at the bottom of the passage seemed to liquefy beneath Chul, and he could feel himself drawn back down the passage. Chul recognized immediately what was happening. Dare was using one of his inventions—a traction impulse device—to suck him back to the cabin. Chips of dirt danced off his shoulders and flitted away toward the hatch.

"Help me, Anita!" he cried. "He's pulling me back!" He tried to grab the sides of the hole, roots, anything, but his grip could find no purchase. Suddenly, he felt a hand reach out of the darkness and seize his.

"Pull hard!" she called from wherever she was and together they fought against the tug of the traction impulse device. Slowly, Chul inched toward the edge of the hole, and, reaching out, he took hold of Anita's other hand. "Pull!" she cried. He dug his feet into the floor of the passage and pushed off with all his might. With a burst of orange and yellow light, he fell through the hole and into another place altogether.

The cold of the passage beneath the cabin in the Two-Hearted Forest was gone, replaced by the hearthside warmth of a huge library of weathered stone, at the center of which stood a round table covered with an ornate carpet. Large and ancient-looking leather-bound books lay open on the table. Beyond, torches burned above niches cut into the walls where statues of what looked to be historical figures stood — a wizened man in Roman laurels, a sorceress in Druidic regalia, an African warrior king, an Iroquois clan mother in beads and a fringed tunic, a turbaned prince in coiled shoes. Below the statutes, the walls were lined with shelves crowded with scrolls and codices. High-backed reed chairs covered with silky cushions stood about. Exhausted, Anita fell into one of these not far from a crackling hearth.

"What is this place?" asked Chul, unsure what was more amazing—the grandeur of the room or their sudden transportation from the dirt-lined tunnel.

"It's Daddy's study," she replied drowsily.

"But I thought you lived in that cabin with your parents."

"Not exactly. That's our summer cabin. Or what's left of it."

"How did we get from there to here?" he asked. "And where *is* here?"

"Oh, that. It's called plinching. Sort of like it sounds. You squeeze two places together for a few seconds and just go through. I don't do it a lot. Mostly…"—she yawned and curled up in the lap of the chair—"because it's *sooo* tiring."

"But…" When he glanced at Anita again, she was fast asleep.

He sensed that they were not alone. He turned and found a man standing at the entrance to the library. "Ah, so are you the young man that wrecked our cabin?"

Chul pointed to Anita. "She started it."

The man smiled. "Yes, she does tend to start things. You'll have to forgive her. We sent her to get you, and it wouldn't do to let you leave. But, then again, we didn't expect your friend Thorium to catch up with you so quickly."

"How do you know Dare?" asked Chul, his surprise increasing every second.

"I knew his father," said the man with distaste. "By the way, my name is Aminou, Georges Aminou. I am Anita's father. Her mother wanted to meet you as well, but she had to step out."

Chul looked at Mr. Aminou carefully. Dare had taught him this sort of thing, how to observe someone to get a sense of their personality and abilities. He found Anita's father pleasant looking but not handsome, strictly speaking. He had a wide, friendly face, frameless glasses, soft skin, and a receding hairline. A man easy to overlook, he thought — and to underestimate.

He put out his hand. "My name is Ch—"

"Chul Sun. Oh, we know much about you, young man. We've been watching you with interest for many years now. Waiting."

"Waiting for what?"

Mr. Aminou smiled. "But, no, I am moving too quickly. Come with me. I have someone who wants to meet you."

At this, Anita woke up and dragged herself up onto her elbow. "Where are you going, Baba?"

Mr. Aminou turned. "Don't you want to sleep, dear?"

"That depends."

"I'm taking him to meet your *Jeddah*."

"Really? I want to come." She bounded to her feet and shook off her sleepiness.

"Who's your *Jeddah*?" asked Chul.

"Oh, you'll see," she said, smiling deviously.

Mr. Aminou and Anita led Chul up a set of stairs out of the library and into a corridor draped with carpets and tapestries. He felt a brace of cold air and, looking up, saw, to his surprise, a seam of stars stretching thick and uninterrupted above. He felt exposed. He had studied books of military tactics that filled the shelves of Dare's library. They warned one to avoid crevasses and holes where one could be attacked from above. *The victor holds the high ground.* Yet, if they were vulnerable here, nothing in the man's posture betrayed any fear. He walked with an easy readiness that Chul, by his training, recognized as physical prowess. His dress was simple—a loose tunic, linen pants, and leather sandals. His only ostentation was a gold ring on the middle finger of his left hand.

"In here," said the man gently, and they turned off of the corridor and descended worn stone steps into a bowl-shaped room draped with flat-woven carpets and crowded about like an indoor forest with ferns, trees, and spikey plants. Looking up, Chul saw a round of the starry firmament and realized, to his dismay, that he was standing in a warren of open ditches and holes. He immediately began to plan his escape from this place. His hand went to his pocket where he touched the velvet-soft edges of the stone he had been carrying with him since his escape from Thorium Dare. He could feel its energy. It was a frightening thing, but also strangely reassuring. In it he could feel the power to destroy him or save him, he knew not which.

As they stepped down into the room, the plants seemed to step in front of them and block their way. Mr. Aminou stopped and put out his hands. "OK, it's me," he said to no one in particular. "*Maman*, where are you? *Maman*?"

"What? Who is it?" came a shrill and wizened

voice, from where Chul could not say.

"It's me, *Maman*. Me and Anita. We brought the boy."

The thicket of vegetation began to tremble before them and then opened, revealing a phalanx of leafy spikes. Mr. Aminou and Anita moved forward, and the spikes drew back, yet remained ominously close, like rows of guards' swords drawn in warning. Chul stayed close behind. He glanced back and saw with alarm the spikes closing behind them. There was no retreat but through a thousand green blades. Even using super speed, he would not be able to get through without being cut to pieces.

"That's close enough, then," said the same sharp voice they had heard before, and Mr. Aminou nodded to Chul to stop where he was.

They were standing in the midst of the thicket. Again, the shrubs shivered and shifted, expelling a twisted trunk of weathered wood. The trunk unfolded and he found to his amazement that this was not a tree at all but an ancient person, her skin twisted and knotted, like a living bonsai. This gnarled little person came closer and stared hard at him out of black, knot-like eyes. Below the nub of a nose, her mouth was drawn up in a slender furrow, but when she spoke, she spoke with surprising force.

"So this is the boy?"

"Yes, *Maman*," said Mr. Aminou.

She sidled closer. "Chul Sun?"

"Yes…" began Mr. Aminou, but she raised a branch to silence him.

"Let the boy speak for himself."

"Yes, ma'am," replied Chul.

"Surprised, aren't you, boy? To be talking to a thing more tree than woman?"

"A little…"

"Three trillion trees on this planet, and did you think there isn't a thinking thing among us? Look. Touch my skin." He put out his fingers and touched the cool, hard seams of her arms. He pulled back his hand. Hers was bark, not skin.

"A bristle cone pine," said Anita. "*Pinus longaeva*, native to Nevada, Utah, and Eastern California. One of the longest living things on the planet. Isn't that right?"

She grinned a row of wood plugs. "Ha! But I'm not all tree, not forever so. I started out as skin and lung, like you. And you could outrun me, sure enough, yes. Speedy young Chul Sun. Fastest child on the planet. Is that how you got away from Thorium Dare? Tell me. By running?"

Chul nodded, struck momentarily dumb by the amount that these people seemed to know about him.

"Yes. He would have caught up with you in the Two-Hearted Forest. The trees tell me you were just minutes away from capture. So we sent Anita to bait you and bring you back here."

"Bait me?"

"Posh! Oh, don't play dullard with me! What young man could resist that girl? I understand you two were fighting like lovers within minutes."

"*Jeddah*!" cried Anita.

The little tree creaked with mirth and turned to Mr. Aminou. "See! He blushes. A good sign. Yes, it was worth the risk. Come now, boy, put your hand in mine, don't be afraid. I won't harm you."

Chul did as he was told. She closed the knots of her eyes. The twigs of her fingers squeezed his hand gently. "Tell me," she asked, "do you feel safe here?"

He glanced up at the roofless void above. "No."

"It is a dangerous world indeed. A dangerous

place. Tell me, are you part of the danger?"

He hesitated, afraid to answer.

The little tree nodded. "That's why he says he adopted you, isn't it? To be dangerous, like him. To put fear into other people's hearts. Chul Sun: The boy that can run faster than lightning and can strike like lightning too! And now that you have run away, you are a danger to him. That is why he will stop at nothing to find you. He will destroy you if necessary. He would destroy *us* to get to you."

Chul began to tremble. He had kept his fear in check since the moment he'd escaped, but this woman was bringing it back again fivefold. He did not like it. He did not want to feel it. He tried to pull away, but her fingers twined like vines around his hands. He pulled harder, but her strength increased with his. He looked to Mr. Aminou and then to Anita. But they merely stood by, not about to interfere with this strange and forceful little tree of a woman.

She re-opened her dark eyes and stared at him fiercely. "Don't pull away. Don't pull away from fear. Don't hide your fear, Chul Sun. Stand with it. Make a home for it. The evil refuse to fear until their fear destroys them. They build up walls around themselves. They build mountain fortresses. They stop at nothing to destroy the thing that makes them fear. What would happen, do you think, if we all succumbed to fear? Why we'd be nothing more than beasts hiding in the hollows, lashing out at the dark. The thing is that we can't…I mean, we must…. Fwah! Georges! What was I saying?"

Mr. Aminou tipped his chin. "*Maman*, the thing in his pocket…"

"But, yes! That! You took something, didn't you? Before you ran away from Dare. What was it?"

Chul's hands were suddenly free. He stepped back, discomposed and astonished. Did he have no secrets from these people?

"I'd rather not say."

"Say."

"It was a key."

"A key," echoed the tree thoughtfully. She put out the branch of her hand. "Show it to me, if you please."

Chul took the thing from his pocket—a thin rectangle of onyx stone. To the untrained eye, it would look like a mobile phone with the power off, yet seamless and engraved around the edges with swirling writing. He handed it to the woman. The twigs of her fingers softened, and she turned it slowly in her grip, murmuring in a language he did not understand.

"*Maman*, is that what I think it is?" asked Mr. Aminou.

"Ah! Yes, son," said the woman. "This is a *khar chuluu*."

"But, I…" began Anita. "What does it do? Is it really a key?"

The old tree eyed her granddaughter shrewdly for a moment and then replied, "What this is is the devil's very own magic. A prodigious magic. A magic to tempt the good to evil. A magic so perfect that it has been banned for three hundred years. Haram is what it is! Haram!" She spat the words at the object. "The question now is where would Dare have gotten this? You, boy, how did you come across this?"

"I found it."

"You found it? Where?"

"I'd rather not say," said Chul.

The old tree seemed about to reply, but changed her mind. She looked up at her son. "What do you think?"

"There are only three places in the world

where he could have gotten this," said Mr. Aminou. "And we know one is safe."

"Safe, yes," said the tree thoughtfully. "So two are safe now."

"Hey!" cried Chul.

The old tree took the *khar chuluu* and pressed it against the bark at her midriff, absorbing the thing into her, like a tree swallowing a spike nailed into its bark. But what would have taken decades for a normal tree happened in seconds. In a few moments, the *khar chuluu* was gone inside of her.

The tree looked sharply at Chul. "Don't think that I have taken something that belongs to you, not forever so. I think you know, young man, that you were in possession of a stolen object, something that belongs to one of the great houses. Besides, where goes the *khar chuluu*...there goes danger." She looked hotly at Anita and then back at Chul. "Mark my words."

And now the little tree was rapidly receding into the thicket from which she had come.

"Now, leave me, all of you. All this human speed wears me out. Out. Out with you!" The semicircle of vegetation opened behind them, and the spikes of leaves nudged Mr. Aminou,

Anita, and Chul back whence they had come.

The trio stumbled out of the thicket and onto the steps that led out of the room into the corridor. Chul had no idea what to make of what had just happened. He felt vulnerable without the *khar chuluu* but then again relieved to be rid of it. He glanced at Mr. Aminou for some sort of explanation.

The man returned his gaze with a calm shrug. "Well, I do believe she likes you."

Chapter 3

*In which Anita the Reckless sneaks
out of the house and conjures a mighty
and dangerous djinn.*

After their visit to the enchanted garden under the stars, Anita showed Chul to his room. As they climbed the stairs away from the sabered palms ranked like soldiers, Anita felt a familiar longing swell inside her. *Jeddah* means grandmother in Arabic, but Anita's grandmother, like the rest of her family, was no ordinary woman. *Jeddah* was a practitioner of the ancient magical arts—the old science. Born with a flame inside her, the same flame that Anita now carried, she had cultivated it, grown it, and learned to harness it. She had done wondrous things. She had fought revolutions; she had romanced kings; she had sailed every ocean and trekked seven continents. This strange woman had taught herself to talk to trees! Speaking to her *Jeddah* was like being in the presence of something forbidding and grand, like a mountain vista or a primeval wood. It made Anita feel very small yet, somehow, full of ambition and primed for adventure.

She led Chul down rough-hewn corridors of yellow stone, the floors and walls smoothed from centuries of sandaled feet and daydreaming fingertips, past the library with its burning sconces and into a suite of rooms. She showed him a small bedroom with a door of Lebanese pine, a carpet, a low bed, a sideboard bearing a bowl of fruit and a stone pitcher of water.

She picked up a magic chamber pot and handed it gingerly to him. "It plinches your doodoo off into the wastes of the desert." He looked down into the thing curiously. "Don't drop anything into it, please. Anything *else*, I mean. Gram — Mamma's mamma — dropped her teeth into one once. We spent half a day picking through dried turds to find them."

Chul looked around the room. "How long will

I be here?"

"I don't know. I guess until Dare stops looking for you."

"He won't stop. I need to get out of here."

"Look," she said, "there are two hundred kilometers of desert in every direction from where we stand. My father's people have lived here for centuries. They know every grain of sand, how to find water, how to deal with sandstorms and the sun. A kid like you doesn't stand a chance out there. My advice: Just stay here where you'll be safe."

Chul didn't respond. He circled the room, inspecting the things. He sniffed the water in the pitcher.

"Do you think we brought you here just to poison you?" she asked. "Is that why you want to escape?"

"Trust no one," he said as he tested the bedding, running his fingers cautiously down the blanket. "That's what Dare taught me. Everyone has a reason for doing what they do."

"You trusted me back at the cabin," said Anita

"Yes, but that was before I knew that you were sent there to get me. Now that tree woman…"

"My *grandmother*…"

"…your grandmother? Well, now she has the *khar chuluu*, or whatever it is, and I am alone in the middle of the what—the Sahara Desert?— with a bunch of strangers. Meanwhile, the world's most dangerous man is hunting me."

"Oh, don't flatter Thorium Dare. He doesn't sound very dangerous to me. *Dude bros* Mamma calls guys like that."

"That's what he wants you to think. You haven't seen what he can do, so you don't know."

Anita watched Chul. He seemed more nervous now than when she had found him in the Two-Hearted Forest. He still hadn't taken off his jacket or shoes. "Can I ask you something?"

"That depends."

"*Jeddah*, she says Dare adopted you. Is he really your dad?"

Chul laughed spitefully. "Yes and no, right? I mean, I thought he was my real dad for the longest time. Until I realized I'm Korean and he's, um, white. At that point, he told me that he's my adopted father. He took me to San Francisco to see the graves of my parents." He paused and seemed to Anita to disappear into some painful memory. And just as quickly, he shook it off. "But now I don't know. I don't know what he is to me.

He could be just the guy that wanted me when no one else did. After all, he was the only one who would take me in after my parents died — because of my…issues."

"Your issues?"

"Yeah, issues. Normal kid stuff like being able to outrun any other human being. Like emitting an electromagnetic pulse strong enough to fry every appliance within ten meters whenever I didn't get my way. The rest of my family were afraid of me and didn't want me. So he took me in. For a long time I was grateful to him. Then I realized he only wanted me for my powers."

"What did he do to you?"

"He lied to me. Used me. Made me rob the Central Bank of Kyrgyzstan. The usual bad parent stuff."

"Did he hurt you?"

"Yes, but *that* I could handle. What I couldn't do was, well..." Chul winced as if feeling a sharp and sudden stab of pain. "He made me hurt other people."

"Is that why you ran away?"

"Part of it," he replied. He stood up on tip-toes as if looking for listening devices in the lamps and along the seams where the walls met the ceiling.

"We don't need bugs to spy on you," said Anita. "You realize that? Mine is one of the most powerful magical families in the world. One of the five ancient houses. You're in good hands."

"If all you can do is turn yourselves into trees and plinch poop out into the desert, I'm in big trouble."

"We *saved* you back there in the Two-Hearted Forest."

"I could have gotten away from Dare again. I did once, I would have done it again. Now why don't you just show me the way out of here so I can be on my way? This place is too exposed. I'd rather take my chances out in the desert than sit around in this *hole*."

"This 'hole' is my father's ancestral home! And no, I'm not showing you the way out. If you want to escape, then you'll have to figure it out yourself. And oh, if you do get out, good luck finding your way back. This place is a lot better protected than you think."

"I'll do fine, thanks," said Chul. "Where are you going?"

"Out," said Anita. "I don't have to stand around while you insult my family. And besides,

I have things to do. So…anyway…good night, or whatever."

"Yeah, whatever."

Anita chuffed away from Chul's quarters feeling sour, a sticky kind of tiredness pulling at her. The soft majority of her wanted to go to her room and fall into bed and sulk, but the restless minority inside would have nothing of it and turned her back down the corridor to the great library, which at this hour was dim and silent, but for the low roll of the fire, kept magically alive so that the proud kings and queens, sorcerers, witches, and chieftains of ancient times standing in the niches about the room would never stare into bald darkness. Anita slipped into the library and could feel them eying her coolly from their perches.

Some people get their superpowers by accident. Some are given them. Others inherit their powers. Anita was in the last category. She belonged to a long line of people with strange and mysterious abilities who had used them over the millennia to do good and ill. Her family was proud that it had done mostly good — except for a few bad apples over the centuries, bad apples like Michaud the Vile, her great, great, great,

great, great uncle, twice removed, who once disappeared an entire village in Brittany; bad apples like Ahmed the Awful, who caused black scarabs to rain down on Baghdad for four days straight in 1083; bad apples like Uvlana the Unutterable who, in 1512, turned every child in Sevastopol into a gray squirrel (most, fortunately, recovered).

But for these notable exceptions, the great, magical people of Anita's family had always used their powers for good, not evil, and had served (and often led) their people with humility and fervor. As one might expect, with such a proud tradition, expectations for her were high, and her ancestors were harsh in their criticism. She had heard them complaining loudly to her father and mother during the times for evaluation, when she was made to stand just outside the door and wait to find out whether she would be allowed to advance to the next level of her training.

"She is powerful, yes," said Gowa once, the druid priestess, "but she lacks self-discipline!"

"I say she's lazy!" groused Ahmed the Awe-Inspiring (not Ahmed the Awful). "She seems to prefer sleeping and playing video games to learning the old arts!"

"Insolent," added the Epicius the Elder, the garlanded Roman. "She lacks proper respect for her father."

Anita's only champion was not made of stone but of wood — her *Jeddah*, who was wheeled into the library in a clay pot for the evaluations. She defended the girl. "You old fools," she growled, "you've spent too long standing in your feet of stone! You've forgotten what it means to be alive and full of real blood — or, in my case, sap. But still!

"You all forget that the trees have memories deeper than the forests. They tell me of a flighty youth named Gowa who turned herself into a breeze and blew all the way to Anatolia in search of a boy. And of Ahmed, the princeling, whose great passion as a child — aside from sherbet — was the game *Halusa*. Little Ahmed, who would not be seen without his *mancala* under his arm! And as for you, Epicius — strange youth! — who defied his own father and fled to Alexandria in search of the fabled diary of Zenodotus! What do you all know about youth? Only everything that you've forgotten!"

And on it would go, the squabbling and the

bickering, until Anita would be readmitted into the library and told that she would be allowed to continue her education. But! She must have more discipline, more energy, more respect.

She tried to have all of these things. But she had trouble focusing, she tired easily, she got angry and talked back to her father and mother. She always felt bad afterwards, but it was hard to control her feelings; they seemed to be as strong as her powers, and she often wished that she were just a normal girl going to school, riding bikes and watching television like all of the other kids she had met in Atlanta when she went to visit her Gram and her mother's family.

But she was not a normal girl. She was anything but: She, Anita Fatima Aminou, was the latest in a line of great and powerful people, a fact that she was never allowed to forget.

She looked up warily at her ancestors around the library, towering in their niches. Everything was quiet, except for the snap of the fire. As casually as she could seem at such a late hour, she made her way across the room, around the great, circular table, to the wall where coiled parchment scrolls rested in dozens of diamond-shaped nooks. She stopped in front and, counting silently, found the one that she was looking for. In that nook there were several scrolls, which she touched one by one in the near darkness, asking silently, *Is it you? Is it you?* Until she felt one of the scrolls reply, *Yes, it's me.* Into this scroll she reached and whispered a simple spell called *aftitah*, a revealing spell that unhid the object that she had hidden in the nook. She felt something fall into her hand, an object of such perfect smoothness that it seemed velveteen, yet impenetrably solid so that it pulled the heat from her fingers. She took it out and looked at in the firelight. The delicate engravings decorating the edges seemed less like writing than like the doodlings of angels. So beautiful. She realized now that she had been foolish to hide this stone in such a conspicuous place, but when she had found it among her grandmother's things, she had not understood what it was or what great powers it may possess. It had been just another gewgaw in her *Jeddah*'s chests and trunks, all left behind when her grandmother first put her feet into soil and began her long transformation from woman to wood.

This was a *khar chuluu*, identical to the one that her *Jeddah* had taken from Chul that evening.

Anita felt a thrill of power run up her arm just to hold it, and as quickly as she could, she tucked the stone into the pocket of her pajamas and hurried out of the library back into the starry corridor.

Once into the corridor and away from the prying eyes of her ancestors, she made sure that the coast was clear. She stepped up to a wall and, waving her hand in a figure eight, she whispered the words, *"daeni 'akhraj"* — let me out — just like her father had shown her. A ladder emerged from the stones that led up and out of the corridor to the dunes above. To a traveler crossing the Saharan wastes or to a lonesome hawk circling above, it would have appeared that Anita had emerged from the sands themselves. A strong magic hid the rooms beneath the desert where she and her family lived. Only a well-trained practitioner of the old science could have sensed the plinch points that allowed one to pass through the sands to the corridors below.

Luckily, these openings were provided by her father's magic, not hers, and Anita came up into the cold, vast night no more winded than she would have been after climbing a flight of steps. She stood under the arc of stars and set her bearings by the Milky Way. Following the lucent stripe of the galaxy, she counted her paces, keeping her hand out in front of her, eyes half-closed, like a diviner. But she was not looking for water. Anita was seeking a hidden place that no one—not her father or her mother or her *Jeddah* or any of her nosey ancestors—knew about. After a few dozen meters, her hands thrilled at the nearness of it. She stopped dead and fell to her knees and inched forward, her concentration full, until she found it.

Any mere human standing next to her would have thought her crazy, on the knees of her pajamas, smoothing the dim sand before her. Once she had smoothed with her palm a pad of sand about one meter by one meter, she drew upon it a perfect circle, her finger guided by a mystical compass, and inside the circle she drew two triangles to form a hexagon, each of its points touching the edge of the circle. This was *Khatam Sulayman*, the Seal of Solomon. And as she drew, she murmured an incantation beneath her breath. "By the Seven Kings I call thee. By Al-Mudhib, I call thee. By Murrah, I call thee. By Al-Ahmar, I call thee." Her voice faded to a whisper, and she felt her whole body tighten with the thrill of great magic and great transgression.

This place, this seal, and this incantation were forbidden to her. Imagine a girl of twelve going to the airport, climbing behind the controls of a Boeing 707, and taking off. Such was the size and severity of the offense that she was committing — and the danger — as she drew the *Khatam Sulayman* and whispered the names of the seven greatest kings of the djinn. "By Barqan, I call thee. By Shamhurish, I call thee."

Suddenly, the sand became like liquid beneath her hand, a pool of deadly quicksand, a trick of divination that had been used in ancient times to snare enemies, but to the wise and skilled *talib*, a way to call forth out of the underrealm the spirits of the desert. Anita kept her body low and flat and, reaching out, furrowed the liquid sand with her fingers, sending out wavelets that glistened under the bright starlight. "By Zoba'ah, I call thee. By Maimun, I call thee."

Awakened, a voice rose from the surface of the sand pool. "Ergh, humph. What? Who is this?"

That voice, dear listeners, was *my* voice. Me. The Mighty and Perspicuous One. Me! The Djinn of All Deserts.

"It is Anita, wise djinn," she replied.

"Anita?" I laughed. "Anita the Child? Anita the Foolhardy? Venturing out into the desert alone at night? Anita the Reckless, casting spells that have killed grown women? Speak if this be you."

She drew a deep breath and stifled her anger. Naturally, she had come to expect this sort of treatment from the Djinn of All Deserts. Me! The Most Powerful Eye. The Eye that Sees the Forty Deserts. Knowledge, alas, is rarely a kindness.

"Yes, it is I, wise djinn," she said, her voice trembling. "I humble myself before you and come to seek your intercourse."

"I was sleeping…"

"Please, wise djinn, I need your help."

"Speak then, silly girl."

"Tell me, wise djinn, where is Thorium Dare?"

"This again?"

"Is he still in the Two-Hearted Forest?"

"No, child, he has left there and travels elsewhere."

"Where, wise djinn? Where is he?"

"In a ship I see him, plying south toward Algiers."

"What is his intent, wise djinn?"

"He seeks the boy, Chul, and the secret thing

the boy possesses. This man, Dare, does not sleep. He comes with grave intent."

"Guide me to him, wise Djinn of All Deserts. Help me to find him."

"Thorium Dare is a dangerous man, no one a child should be seeking! I should tell your father."

"But you can't, wise djinn."

"And why is that?"

"I bind thee, wise djinn. I bind your magic to me, and to me your secrets will be bound. You will have no memory of me to my father or my mother."

"Argh! Who taught you that? What books have you been reading? I tell you, Anita the Reckless! You dabble in frightful magic and seek a frightful man. I shan't do it!"

"I bind thee, wise djinn. By the *Khatam Sulayman*, I bind thee." She stroked the fluid stands. "Guide me to Thorium Dare."

"You will surely die."

"Guide me, wise djinn!"

"Anita the Cunning! Know this! I can guide you, but I cannot protect you. Don't imagine that you will be able to lead Thorium Dare into some clumsy trap of quicksand. He may seem like a fool to you, but he has studied arts of which you have no comprehension. He has no mercy or pity within him. I fear that his rage is greater than your ambition."

Anita continued to stroke the surface of the fluid sand and completed the spell that was to bind me. "By Al-Mudhib, I bind thee. By Murrah. By Al-Ahmar. By Barqan, Shamhurish, Zoba'ah and Maimun, I bind thee, wise djinn! You shall guide me over the desert to this man."

It was done. "I am bound and now serve you, master," said I. "A spell that only death can break. *Your* death, mind you. Not mine, for I am the Djinn of All Deserts, and I have served many masters, some wise, some fools, some cunning or cruel. They have all died, in one way or another, and yet I live and burn beneath midday sands. I pile into storms, I sleep centuries and play across the continents like you play in your bedroom. Do you understand me?"

But Anita the Reckless paid no attention. She stirred herself up from the sand and brushed off her pajamas. A mixture of fear and resolution gripped her. Dare was on his way to Algiers and there was no time to lose. She retraced her footsteps to the plinch point and climbed down into the corridor. She made her way to her room where she had already tucked away in a dresser drawer everything she would need for a journey: a hat, a backpack, a khaki shirt, and pants. She changed into her desert clothes, laced her boots, packed water and provisions, and cinched the backpack on her shoulders. She removed the *khar chuluu* from her pocket. She could feel its dark magic radiating around it. She did not know what it did, but she knew of a man that could tell her, and she sensed that with this black stone and the Djinn of All Deserts she could find and defeat Thorium Dare. She had come one step closer to proving her worth to her father and her mother, to her *Jeddah,* to all her stony ancestors, and, most of all, to herself.

Chapter 4

*In which Chul Sun escapes from safety
and chases Anita the Reckless – and
a real-life magic carpet – all the way
to Algiers.*

After Anita had left his room, Chul lay cautiously down in the bed and stared at the ceiling. Despite his abuse, Thorium Dare had taught him a thing or two. One of which was to carefully assess one's situation and act with cool and decisive calculation. Another thing was to survive, if necessary, on very little sleep. He set his watch to sixty minutes and woke up to a beeping that seemed to erupt the moment he had closed his eyes. He swung his feet to the ground and set himself in motion.

The corridor was empty when Chul stepped out, lit by a line of torches burning intermittently. Looking up, he saw that the vault of stars had slid westward while he slept. He guessed it about an hour before first light. He was not certain where exactly he was but supposed that the Aminou house was somewhere in the Saharan Desert, in North Africa, which meant that the Mediterranean Sea lay to the north. So north he would go. Running at top speed, he could be well away by daylight. He would hunker down in the heat of the day and then move on again at nightfall. By next morning, he thought, he could reach civilization and some port town from which he could make his way north again.

Backing up, he took a run at the wall. He vaulted up its stone face—which was easy to do if you ran as fast as Chul Sun—and expected to launch himself out onto the sands above. Instead, he was rudely rebuffed and went tumbling back to the ground. He stood up and dusted the bottom of his trousers. "What the—" He stepped back and cocked his head, looking. He could not see what he might have run into. Watching carefully this time, Chul took a second run at the wall. The same thing happened again. It was as if he had bounced off a pane of glass, but there was no glass to be seen, just the open sky. He could even feel the cool desert air sinking into the corridor.

While Chul was puzzling over this turn of events, he heard someone approaching. Jumping into super speed, he darted around the corner. And looked. It was Anita, coming from the other direction and, curiously, no longer dressed in her pajamas but wearing a backpack, khakis, suede boots, and a floppy, wide-brimmed hat. She had a teal carpet rolled up under her arm. He watched as she waved her hand in a figure eight in front of the wall and murmured a brief incantation. The wall seemed to liquefy and from it emerged a series of ladder rungs that set to solid stone.

She climbed the ladder and scrambled onto the sands. And then, somehow, she stepped right back over the gap above the corridor as if walking on thin air. Chul waited for a minute or two, then went over to the place where she had been standing. He had keen hearing and Dare had taught him the arts of mimicry—a parrot-like ability to repeat back words and sounds that he had heard, even if he didn't know what they meant. He waved his hand in the same figure eight and repeated the incantation he had heard Anita recite. *Daeni 'akhraj.* He thrilled to see the ladder appear out of the wall. He stepped onto the first rung and, finding it solid, climbed up. Coming out, he found himself surrounded by a vast stretch of desert. The land, dimly lit under the stars, fell off to the horizon like the cracked skin of a burnt cake. There were no signs of the corridors, halls, rooms or gardens beneath him. Just sand and rocks. So this, he thought, was why the Aminous were so confident striding about below.

Chul stepped away from the plinch point, careful to avoid Anita's foot prints, and walked in a wide arc to set his bearings. The night sky, unbesmirched by city light, sprawled brightly above him, a sea of stars, the galaxy slow-crashing like a juggernaut into the westward scape of desert. To Chul Sun, the sky was all this, but also a map, and his eyes instantly sought, and found, the pivot point of the firmament— Polaris—hanging dim and low just over the horizon. North. From his earliest memories, he had done this by night, searching out the pole star as if by instinct. He tethered himself to it, so that even with his eyes closed, he could slew himself toward it like a gyroscope. And a saying filtered into his memory, from where he did not know: "A person who knows the Earth is never truly lost." This was not something Dare had taught him. It was a wisdom he simply *knew*, and it gave him comfort. Chul cinched his backpack and readied himself to set out over the desolate landscape before him.

"Where do you think you're going?"

He turned. It was Anita. He was surprised that she had been able to sneak up on him, but then, he thought, he should have known given how she had seemed to anticipate his movements back in the cabin. "Nowhere," he said. "Where are *you* going?"

"Nowhere."

"Looks like we're both going nowhere."

"Seriously," said Anita, "it's dangerous out here. You'll be much safer down in the house. You can see now that it's a hidden place. Down below, you can see the sky because of an enchantment. It lets us see out, but other people can't see in."

"I can't stay here," said Chul. "I told you. Dare is looking for me. I'm not going to wait around here sitting on my hands while I put your family in danger."

"But where are you going to go?"

"Away," he said. "Maybe I'll find my way back to America." In reality, he planned to go directly back to the Two-Hearted Forest, but he wasn't going to tell her this. He didn't want her, or anyone, to know that he intended to go back there, let alone to know what he was looking for. *He* wasn't even sure what he was looking for. All the more reason to keep it a secret.

"That doesn't sound like much of a plan," said Anita. "Do you even know where you are?"

"Of course. By the name of your father and the style of your home, I am guessing this is North Africa, a former French territory, Algeria or Tunisia. So if I go due north I will hit the coastline—Tunis or maybe Algiers—and from there I can sneak onto a ferry."

"You can't go north like that," replied Anita, a hint of panic slipping into her voice. "You can't go to Algiers."

"Why not?"

"You just can't go to Algiers, is all."

"You know, when you say to somebody, 'Don't go to Algiers,' they're going to go to Algiers. It's like saying, 'Don't think of a pink elephant.'"

"It's a lot easier to think of a pink elephant than to go to Algiers."

Chul laughed. "Not for me. I'm pretty speedy, remember. So why can't I go to Algiers?"

"Because I said so. Because it's dangerous."

"More dangerous than the Two-Hearted Forest?"

"Yes…I mean, for you. I mean, yes. Please, just don't go there. Do you even have water?"

"You're changing the subject."

"It's a *desert*. People die out here. Do you have water?"

"Some," he said. "You still think I can't take care of myself, don't you?"

"No, I don't. And I'm not sure I care. What I do know, though, is that my mom and dad risked a lot—namely *moi*—to bring you here, and now you are going to cut and run, which seems pretty selfish to me."

"Ah! OK, I'm selfish. What about you? Why don't we go ask your parents what they think? I'm sure they would be very curious to see you dressed to trek the desert in the dead of night…"

"You can't do that!"

"That's what I thought," said Chul. "So, if

you're not going to tell me where you're going then I'm not going to tell you where I'm going."

"You know what, Chul Sun, I have half a mind to whoop your butt, just like I did back in the cabin, and drag you down into the house."

"What? You didn't whoop my butt."

"I whooped your butt, mister…"

"…pfft, I was so whooping you…"

"…young man! I served you up such a big ol' slice of whoop-butt…"

They were going on like this when they heard a scuffling behind them. Someone poked their head up out of the plinch point. "Who's that? Is there someone up here?"

Anita grabbed Chul's jacket sleeve and dragged him down the slope of a dune and out of sight. She whispered, "That's Siddiq, the housekeeper. Jeez. You don't think he saw us do you?"

Chul didn't answer. The moment Anita released his hand, he bolted away at super speed, so fast that he didn't leave any tracks in the sand. He didn't stop until he was a half a kilometer away. He collected himself and looked back regretfully. He didn't like leaving like that, without even saying goodbye, but he couldn't afford to be caught by the housekeeper and taken back into the house. He needed to return to the Two-Hearted Forest as soon as possible, which meant leaving without further ado. What was in the Two-Hearted Forest he could not say, but he knew it was important. Somewhere, he sensed, in that cold wilderness was hidden the key of who he was and where he had come from. He hitched his backpack and took off, running north at a steady lope.

The still desert air turned into a wind across his face. Chul could run at eighty kilometers an hour for hours on end, and his strides stretched into graceful bounds. He thrilled from the ground rush, skipping gently off the ground, leaving puffs of dust in his wake. He headed straight north, following Polaris. It was easy going in the cool desert night, but a thought kept pestering him. Where was Anita going? And why didn't she want him to go to Algiers? What did she know that she wasn't telling him? But that was none of his business, right? The whole point was to get *away* from these people, to put them out of danger and not get caught up in their affairs. But, argh! Where in the world *was* she going? And why?

Chul began to slow. He stopped. He turned around and looked southward from where he had come. Dawn was just a chalk line to the east but growing steadily brighter, so that he could now make out, from the rise upon which he stood, the undulant variations in the landscape. The night-moistened earth had a sagey balm to it. A falcon circled above, and he made out, with his keen hearing, the skirl and skitter of night creatures finding refuge below ground. Following suit, Chul sank to the earth beneath the lip of the rise and hunkered down. He watched south, waiting for her.

Just after daybreak, he saw something very peculiar. Was it a mirage?

First a trickle, now a stream, then a flood, the sand seemed to liquefy, turning into a river running north like a second Nile, roiling the rocks aside. The sand river sliced the ground over rise and into trough, like the back of a desert snake, smelling ancient and musty, murmuring, grumbling, and grousing as it passed. And as soon as it passed, the river of sand closed in upon itself and left no trace. And then, above and behind, riding like a kite behind the river, Chul saw the wimpling edge of a teal carpet floating high in the sky. And upon the carpet was…Anita! Though far above him, with his sharp eyes Chul could see her seated cross legged, arms crossed, with the imperious eye of a sultana. Not once did she remove her downcast eyes from the moving river of sand. They moved swiftly as one — river, carpet, and girl — and in a few minutes, they were gone, rushing north toward the sea.

Where was that girl going? Algiers, maybe?

Despite the mounting heat and without hesitation, Chul rolled up his blanket and took off after Anita in his steady, bouncing lope.

All day, Chul chased her across the land. The closer to civilization they came, the higher she rose, and the more varied became the course of the strange, sentient river. They circled around villages, encampments, and army outposts. He resorted to short, blinding bursts of speed from hill to hill to evade notice. And by afternoon, the boulevards, buildings, and brightly colored billboards of Algiers came into view.

Chul pulled his blanket over his head and tried to look anonymous as Anita came down with the carpet in a back alley of the city and rolled up her conveyance under her arm. The river of sand that had roiled the desert shrank down and was now just a fillip of distortion at her foot, like a shard of a heat mirage that had broken off and joined her at her heel.

Anita tied a *hijab* around her chin and slipped on a long skirt, and with her pink scarf and floral backpack looked for all the world like an ordinary Algerian school girl walking home from the *lycée*. In fact, Chul almost missed her as she emerged from the alley into the babble and richly spiced odors of the city street. She turned and walked away with purpose, her expression fierce and focused. He watched her until she was almost out of sight. From the storefronts wafted the smell of lamb and warm flat bread, stoking his hunger, but he fought that down. There was no time to lose by eating. He slipped into the crowd and followed the resolute course of Anita the Reckless.

Chapter 5

*In which Anita the Reckless searches
for the secret of the* khar chuluu *in an
Algiers electronics store only to be
scolded by her very own father.*

"Thorium Dare isn't here, master," crooned
a voice at Anita's feet. That was me
speaking—the Djinn of All Deserts—
reduced to a helpless flicker of heat floating at the
girl's heel. A humiliating form, I must admit, but
a djinn bound is helpless against his master, and
she might as well have commanded me to be a
dog on a leash, so lowly was my state. Yet as a
dog will whine and raise his hackles, even the
mighty Djinn of All Deserts was not above
trolling his master. "He is leagues from here,

crossing the sea."

"I know," replied Anita curtly, scanning the storefronts and vendors' stalls.

"Have you lost heart?" said I. "Have you maybe decided to stop your foolish quest to get yourself killed?"

"I've done nothing of the sort!"

"But why have you come here? I told you to avoid the city. It is a bothersome place. If you want Dare, I'm sure you won't find him in a shirt store or a toy shop. Ah! Maybe it is a nice toy you are looking for? A plastic baby doll, perhaps?"

"Are you always this insufferable to your masters?" growled the girl.

"Oh, I have respected a master or two," said I. "There was Sulayman himself, and his namesake Sulayman the Magnificent. Ah! Now those were men of power and distinction, men worthy of the name 'master.' Yes, and then there was—"

"Shut up!" snapped Anita, and I shut up. Alas, a djinn bound must always respect the command of his master, no matter how feckless she may be. And so I floated along, a helpless, gagged scrap of heat, and watched the girl as she wandered the city streets.

Nervousness and frustration had clouded

Anita's perceptions. She needed to focus, to push out my voice and the noise around her. She stopped on the street in front of a brightly lit and blinking mobile phone store, closed her eyes and breathed deeply, pushing out everything. Like her Gram in Atlanta had taught her, she sought out the quiet place inside her. She pictured herself standing in a wide, green field, where the only sound was the hush of the wind blowing through the grass. Everything became calm and she could sense, radar-like, the closeness of the man she was seeking—a man named Mohammed Kateb, the renowned repairer of magic devices. Her intuition had steered her to the right place. She felt her confidence returning.

But then Anita sensed someone else. Another presence she knew. She snapped around angrily and marched across the street to an alleyway tucked dimly between the bright shop fronts on either side.

"You!" She reached into the alley and pulled the blanket off of Chul's head. "What are you doing here?"

He stepped out of the alley, looking like a boy caught with his hand in the cookie jar. "Shopping?"

"As if!" snarled Anita. "You followed me here."

"I was worried about you."

"Worried about *me*? I'm two years older than you, Chul Sun. You know what I think? I think you just came here to spy on me. I knew I should have gone to my father the minute you escaped."

He shrugged complacently. "You still can. I'm sure we can find a phone if you want to give him a call…"

"Never mind," hissed Anita.

Chul just smiled, pointing to the teal roll beneath her arm. "Was that really a flying carpet I saw you on?"

"What? Yes. My family has used them for centuries. Hardly anybody uses them anymore. Silly-looking things."

"And what was that thing you were following? That river of sand?"

"Nothing," said Anita.

"*NOTHING?*"

Chul looked around for the voice. "Who said that?" The voice was mine, naturally, the mighty and ancient Djinn of All Deserts, forced to listen to children prattle.

"Ignore that voice," said Anita. "It's just an

exasperating djinn."

"THE DJINN OF ALL DESERTS!" said I. "And this, young man, is Anita the Reckless, the foolish girl who has decided to chase after Thorium Dare."

"Chase after Dare?"

Anita pulled Chul into the alley. "I told you to ignore him!"

"Anita, you can't do that! Dare is a crazy man. Believe me, I know. He only cares about two things: power and, well, more power. He knows no mercy. He only treated me well because I was useful to him."

"That's why someone has to stop him," said Anita.

"Who's someone? You?"

Anita stiffened. "Maybe. Why not?"

"Because it's crazy. That's why. The djinn is right. You'll get killed. You need to go back home."

"No. I mean, I think there's a way. Look…with this." Anita pulled off her backpack and removed the smooth black stone about the size of a cell phone. It glimmered briefly under the shop lights.

"The *khar chuluu*!" said Chul. "How did you

get it? I thought your grandmother took it and stuck it into her trunk...or her stomach...or whatever she did with it."

"It's not the same one that she took from you. You see, she had one. *Jeddah* did. She had a *khar chuluu* in her things. I found it years ago one day when I was looking through her stuff. Really, I wasn't supposed to, but she has all of this cool, ancient stuff that has been sitting around in her rooms ever since she started to become a tree. So anyway, I was looking through one of her trunks one day when I found this. It was just, I don't know, just beautiful to look at. I know I shouldn't have taken it, but I did, and I hid it in the library and then sort of forgot about it. I just never realized that it was a magical key."

"It's not a key," said I.

"What?" said Anita.

"The *khar chuluu* is not a key, fool girl. Who told you that?"

"Dare said it was a key," said Chul.

"Then Dare is a fool like the both of you. The *khar chuluu* is a wicked thing, full of dark magic, an object banned on Earth since the Tripoli Conclave of 1719, but it is NOT a key."

"Then what is it?" asked Chul.

"Not for me to say."

Anita hissed, "I bind you, Djinn of All Deserts."

"Grrr, OK. It's an embodiment object. It allows the user to become any person they please."

"What? You mean like a disguise?" asked Chul. "Like looking like another person? What's the big deal with that?"

"What's the big deal? Fool boy! The *khar chuluu* is not just some trifling impersonation charm. I can take the shape of either of you, but I can only *look* like you. Any magical person worth their salt would be able to tell it was a trick. Oh, no. The *khar chuluu* allows you to *become* another person—body, soul, and mind. You have access to all of their thoughts, memories, everything. The greatest magicians of all time have not been able to detect the transformation made possible by the *khar chuluu*."

"How does it work?" asked Chul.

"Don't ask me," said I. "I don't truck in human magic."

Anita said, "That's why we're here. There is someone who I think will know."

"Who's that?" asked Chul.

"You'll find out. Follow me."

Anita took Chul by the wrist and crossed the street. The shop lights had grown bright against the deepening dusk, a darkling amethyst stretched tight over the street, cut through with bands of orange. The cool drew crowds out into the city night. The two children dodged cars and people until they reached the store that Anita was looking for. It was fronted by a narrow window crowded with zithers and lights, a riot of LEDs, blinged-out mobiles, and golden phone accessories draped like the dowry of a desert princess. Inside, the patrons were mostly older boys with floppy hair, jeans, sneakers, and hoodies all hunched over phones and touch pads. These devices were built using what the ancient families like Anita's called the *new science* — the science of electricity, semi-conductors, photons, silicon, and electromagnetic waves — that over the centuries had come to eclipse the old science. Most of the people in the street didn't even believe in magic at all. Staring up at these prodigies in the window, Anita wondered who could blame them. In ancient times, only the most powerful witch or wizard could talk to someone on the other side of the world. Now, anybody could.

The floppy-haired boys eyed up Anita and Chul as they walked in and then went back to what they were doing. A scruffy boy of about fourteen was seated behind the counter in a keffiyeh and earbuds, mumbling French rap as he pecked the keyboard of his laptop. Anita stood in front of him for a good twenty seconds before he bothered to look up and yank the earbuds out from under his shaggy hair. He was sprouting the beginnings of a mustache.

"Yeah?" said the boy.

"I need help," said Anita.

"What do you want? A phone case? We don't got Hello Kitty or Tin Tin or any of that crap."

"I don't want a phone case. I'm looking for Mo Kateb. "

"Which one?" said the boy.

"Which one?"

"Yeah, which one? There are two of us that work here. Me and my dad."

"I want your dad."

"He's in the back."

"Can you go and get him?"

"What do you want him for?"

"Look," Anita said, pulling the *khar chuluu* from her pocket and setting it down on the glass counter. "I'm trying to figure out how to use this."

"You don't know how to use your phone?"

"It's *not* a phone."

Only then did the boy look at the thing that Anita had put on the counter, really *look* at it. He did a double-take and jumped right up off his stool. He stared at Anita as if she had just sprouted horns from her head. He backed away toward the door behind the counter and wagged his finger. "You. You stay there. Don't go anywhere."

The boy disappeared into the back room, and a moment later an older man with a bald pate, round glasses, and leather jacket stepped out. "You there," he said to Anita, "I heard you are looking for me."

"Yes."

He glanced at the object on the counter. "Why have you come here?"

"The *khar…*" she began, but he held up a finger in warning.

"I don't know what you've heard, but I think it's best that you leave right now." And then, suddenly, the man flew around the counter. For a terrified moment, Anita thought he was going to attack her, but he stopped short and stared at Anita's feet. "Did you bring a djinn into my store?"

"THE DJINN OF ALL DESERTS!" said I, still just a shard of heat at Anita's heel. The mop-top boys all around the shop leaped comically, dropping their touch screens and cell phones. They all stared at Anita, thinking that she was the one who had said this.

The man, Mo Kateb, turned to the boys. "Out! All of you!"

The boys poured into the street. As soon as they were gone, Mo snapped his fingers. The blind at the front window clamped down tight and the doors locked fast. We were alone—the five of us—Anita, Chul, the two Mo Katebs (younger and older), and of course, yours truly, the all-seeing and mighty Djinn of All Deserts.

"Who are you?" demanded Mo of Anita. She watched him. As she had done with Chul back in the cabin, she probed his intentions. She could detect no malice in Mo Kateb, just curiosity mixed with alarm. She sensed him worrying too—but his worry was not for himself. His worry was for her and Chul Sun.

"Yasmine," she replied. "And this is my

friend, um, Daniel."

"That's not their names!" said I.

"Shut up!" barked Anita.

"Just saying…"

"Be quiet!"

"It sounds like you can't control this djinn of yours," said Mo Kateb. "Why don't you show him to me so I don't have to listen to your foot."

"Show yourself, Djinn of All Deserts." At this, I piled myself up into a grizzled old man, my favorite form.

Mo looked from Anita to Chul and back again. "Do your parents know where you two are right now?"

She took out ten one-hundred-euro bills—more than a thousand dollars American—and set them on the counter. "I was told you don't ask questions."

Mo looked at the money but did not touch it. His lips withered to a line. "What do you want?"

"I want to know how to work this." Anita nodded to the object on the counter.

Mo didn't even look at it. "What? It's a cell phone."

"No, it isn't," she said. "You know what it is."

The younger Mo craned his neck for a closer

look. "How did she get one, Dad?"

"They exist," said the older Mo brusquely as he eyed up Anita. "Three, to be exact. In the old families. The rest are frauds." He stepped forward and carefully picked up the *khar chuluu* from the counter and ran his thumb over the bright black surface. He turned to his son. "If it's a counterfeit, it is a good one. No seams. Just the right weight. The markings appear to be authentic, etched without flaw."

"How can you tell if it's a fake?" asked the younger Mo.

"There is only one way to tell, really. And that requires violating the Tripoli Conclave of 1719."

"What's the Tripoli Conclave?" asked Chul.

"Well," said Mo, "if this is what your friend — *Yasmine* — thinks it is, then it is one of only three known to be in existence. Each of the *khar chuluu* was made more than three hundred years ago by a man named Eno Timur. Timur was a passable alchemist in his day, but his real talent was teasing the magical properties out of ordinary things. A shoe, a spoon, a rock. Timur saw that everything has a kind of magic, a kind of energy in it, some of it weak, some of it very strong, and he learned over the years, by trial and error, how to turn this energy from potential to kinetic, in so many words. This was part of the old science, before the new science came along. Most of it is forgotten."

Mo turned the *khar chuluu* in his hand. "Yes, but unfortunately, Eno Timur, like many men with great talents, was also a troubled man. He struggled against demons, both real and imagined. These demons goaded him to do more and more audacious things, dangerous things, unnatural things. And here we have the result. The *khar chuluu*."

"The forbidden art," I added, wagging a withered finger. "A dark magic."

"A magic, yes," said Mo, "whether dark or not depends on the hand it falls into. But it was clear to the great families that some objects are too powerful to be trusted to the fates and the good intentions of the generations. After Timur's tragic death, the families convened in Tripoli and decided to ban the use of the *khar chuluu* forever."

"Banned," dreamily echoed the younger Mo Kateb. He stared awestruck at the legendary stone. Indeed, the *khar chuluu* was a most fascinating object.

"Why didn't they just get rid of them?" asked

Chul.

"Ah, yes, that," said Mo. "The *khar chuluu* cannot be destroyed. No magic known can break them or take away their powers. So three of the great families of the time each took one for safekeeping. Forever, it was supposed. But now it seems one has left the protection of the great families and has fallen into the hands of... children." Mo stared at Anita meaningfully.

"So, tell us," said the younger Mo, "how can you tell if it's a fake or not?"

"You have to use it," replied the older Mo. "That's the only way." He contemplated the *khar chuluu*. Anita could sense his intense curiosity and the thrill of holding such a powerful thing. "But then again," he said, "some people say that the Tripoli Conclave went out of effect in 1918 when Kelnick Dare betrayed the five families."

"If it is banned," asked Chul, "how do you know how to work it?"

Mo Kateb smiled slyly. "You could say that my magical education was *thorough*. My family has passed down the secrets of the old science for generations, even the forbidden ones."

"So you *do* know how to use it!" said Anita, her excitement mounting.

"Of course."

Anita could sense his feelings, his conflict. He was sorely tempted to use the stone. She said, "Test it, Mr. Kateb. Show us if it's real."

"Yeah, Dad," said the younger Mo, "test it!"

"If you do," Chul asked, "can you become anyone in the world? Even King Tut or Napoleon?"

"No, no," said Mo. "It has to be a living person. You see, the *khar chuluu* allows you to embody another person completely. Napoleon and King Tut are dead so there is nothing to embody. Just dust. And in order to become that living person, you need something that is loved and desired by the person."

"I love my backpack," offered Anita.

Mo shook his head. "No! No idle preoccupation. No short-lived desires. This has to be something someone has loved and desired with the fullness of their spirit. Ah, I have it!" He gripped the *khar chuluu* and in a swift motion seized Anita's wrist. She tried to pull away, but could not. It was not Mo's strength that held her, but some other power. She could feel it coming from the *khar chuluu* itself.

With his free hand, Mo pressed the *khar chuluu*

against his chest, and still holding fast to Anita's wrist, launched into a rapid incantation that she could not follow.

At once, his body began to warp and shimmer. And, like sometimes you see in a dream where one person suddenly becomes another, Mo became Georges Aminou. And he did not merely look like Georges Aminou. He *was* Georges Aminou. Anita felt this down to the marrow of her bones. In her mind, heart, and soul. Standing before her was her very own father. And it terrified her.

"Anita, why did you come here?" he asked, his voice full of pain and anger. "Why did you leave home without a word?" She pulled her arm out of his hand and backed away and hit the opposite wall. She began to sputter, helplessly. "I...I'm..."

"And you have bound this djinn! How could you do such a thing?"

"I'm sorry..."

"We are so disappointed in you, Anita."

"I'm sorry, Baba. I'm sorry! I'm sorry!"

"That's enough!" snapped Chul. "You're scaring her. Stop!"

In the same confused and dreamy way, Georges Aminou became Mo Kateb again. When

Anita had recovered herself, Mo spoke, this time as himself. "Now that you have seen the power of this thing, maybe I should tell you what became of Eno Timur.

"For many years, Timur worried about having a child to carry on his work. In his old age, he and his wife settled in Bratislava outside the walls of the old fortress. For years, try as they might, they had been unable to have a child. So Timur took on an apprentice, a boy not much older than the two of you. He began to teach the boy alchemy and pass on the secrets of the old science. He was fond of the apprentice, but still he longed for a child of his own.

"Then one day, Timur's wife came to him and told him that she was going to have a child. Like Zechariah, Timur's prayers had been answered. Soon Timur and his wife had a baby, a little boy they named Vanya, and they were filled with joy. They loved Vanya with all their hearts and souls. And now that they had a real son, Timur turned the apprentice out and sent him back to the home of his parents.

"But this apprentice was a cunning and ambitious boy, and, burning with jealousy, he waited for his moment to get his revenge. Vanya grew into a bright and precocious boy. He loved animals. And for Vanya's fifth birthday, Timur gave the boy a little gray duckling still in its down. Vanya loved the duckling. He fed the duckling and played with the duckling. He even slept with the duckling in his bed.

"One morning, the bird went missing. Vanya ran into the forest to look for it. Later that morning, he returned home with the duckling. Timur and his wife were so happy to see the boy that they rushed to the door to greet him. But as they did, the boy drew a dagger from his cloak and thrust it into the chest of his father. He did the same to his mother. The people of the village, seeing this happen, went mad with grief and horror. But this boy, little Vanya, showed not a whiff of emotion. He simply dropped the dagger and the duckling on the front steps of his home and walked away as calmly as you please back into the forest.

"When the people of the village had recovered from their shock, they ran into the forest after the boy. They soon found the little boy, wandering about, still calling out the name of the duckling. The old science was as little understood then as it is now. The people thought the boy was possessed by the devil and demanded he be locked in the dungeon in the castle above the Danube, where he spent many years.

"Learning of the terrible death of Eno Timur, representatives were sent by the five families to investigate. Suspicion turned immediately to the apprentice, but no *khar chuluu* was found in his possession. All three stones were found in the home of Eno Timur. The magical families could never prove the wicked apprentice was responsible for this terrible act. Meanwhile, in the darkness and isolation of the dungeon, the little boy Vanya came to believe that it was truly he who had killed his parents. He slowly went insane from grief and guilt and loneliness. He died just a few years later.

"You see, the power of the *khar chuluu* is unparalleled in the old science. A moment ago, I was able to, in a sense, become your father. I knew everything he knew. I had all his thoughts and memories. But I was also in control, like a daemon in a machine. This was how that wicked apprentice was able to deceive and murder Eno Timur and his wife while their son wandered the forest." Mo dropped the *khar chuluu* onto the counter with a thud. "And that is why these things were banned. This is not a magic to be taken lightly."

Anita had recovered from her shock. Slowly, her intellect reminded her that she had not truly seen her father, only a perfect duplicate. The *khar chuluu* had allowed the older Mo to look exactly like him. Mo could access his thoughts and memories. He could even control the body he inhabited, but her real father was miles away, in the family home under the desert sands. Thinking this through, it seemed to her that the story of Eno Timur, as terrible as it was, was something that could never happen to her. She would never use the *khar chuluu* in that way.

"So will you show me how to use it?" she asked.

"No," replied Mo Kateb in disbelief.

"Why not?"

"Have you not heard anything I've said?"

Anita reached into her bag and took out ten more one-hundred-euro bills. More than two thousand U.S. dollars now lay on the counter beside the ancient object. Anita could sense Mo's temptation to take the money. He looked at the stack ruefully. "Where did you get this money?"

"For someone who doesn't ask questions, you

ask an awful lot of questions," said Anita.

He shook his head wearily. "Between the five great houses, my family has been neutral for two centuries, and I don't think it would be wise for me to make an enemy of Georges Aminou." He pushed the money and the *khar chuluu* toward Anita. "Come back when you are of age. If time and magic have corrupted you, then it will be your doing. Until then, I won't be responsible for your downfall. Even for all that money."

In a flash, the blinds snapped back up and the street life resumed on the sidewalk outside — the bustle of an ordinary evening. The mop-top boys filtered back into the shop, toying with their cell phones like nothing had happened. And the older Mo Kateb was gone, the counter empty. Anita felt a stab of panic, and reaching into her pocket, she found both the money and the *khar chuluu* where they had been when she had entered the shop.

The younger Mo Kateb returned to his stool behind the counter. He put in his ear buds and glanced warily at Anita and Chul. "You two should probably go."

Chapter 6

In which the considerable eye of the Djinn of All Deserts finds Thorium Dare bedridden, in a boat, crossing the dark sea.

A question for you, good listener, before we proceed: If you could look in on anyone at any time, would you look? Would you hover in the air invisible and listen in on your mom or dad in hopes of hearing your name? Would you try to find out what you might get for your birthday? Would you spy on your teacher come Saturday to see what kind of pajamas she wears? Or more than this: Would you sneak onto the playground to spy on your friends to see what they say about you? If you

85

had such a power, could you resist? Would curiosity overtake you? Or would you be afraid of what you might learn?

No human to whom I have been bound has been able to resist the pull of curiosity. Humans live in such a shroud that they will do anything to have a peek out, even if what they learn will destroy them. Yet I, the great and mighty Djinn of All Deserts, having just such a power, lost anything remotely like curiosity thousands of years ago. I find human beings terribly boring, I must admit, with all their shilling for money and fighting and falling in and out of love and bragging about little Malik or Marie and how well they did in the football match or in their marks at school. So boring.

As for Anita the Reckless, I found her no better than the rest of them, burning with her own self, blinded by her desire to prove herself and put down her small mark in the book of human history. And I would not even have bothered to cast my considerable eye toward Thorium Dare had she not bound me. For what was this man to me or me to him? Better to stay out of human affairs, I say, and let those made of clay fight amongst themselves. But, yet again, the Seal of

Sulayman had bound me to one of them and to her schemes.

Anita was my master, and when she commanded me, I had no choice but to look, and from an alleyway in the Bab El Oued of Algiers, my vision wandered north, across the dark sea to a bobbing junk plying south from Marseilles, an old rust bucket flying a French flag and puttering anonymously — under the radar, so to speak. The sailors on the merchant ships and fishing boats passing in the cold, starless night could not have guessed that aboard this ship was the last in the line of a family that had broken from the five great magical families nearly a century before, a young man who burned to reclaim the glory of a faded name, who burned to someday rule the world — a man named Thorium Dare.

My eye found him in a dim and cramped ship's cabin heavy with the odor of menthol. Bushy-haired, no more than twenty-five, despite his surf shop wardrobe and suntan, he was actually rather small and sickly. He was heaped red-eyed and ashen on a pile of blue silk pillows, each monogrammed with T.A.D. for Thorium Aloysius Dare. He tugged at his stubbish nose with a quilted tissue and scowled at the two men standing before him.

"You know, there's like one thing in this stinking, puny world I hate more than anything. You, Cribb! What do you think it is?"

Cribb winced at the sound of his name. Whenever a Dare asked a question like that, it was best to act dumb. "I don't rightly know."

"Of course you wouldn't. How about you, Mossmuss? Do you got a clue?"

"None whatsoever."

Dare pursed his lips, began to say something, but then let out a head-splitting sneeze. He waved his hand around desperately. Mossmuss, the larger of the two, fished about the room. He produced an inhaler, which Dare waved off furiously, and then a box of lozenges, which Dare slapped out of his hand, and then a Kleenex box, which Dare snatched up and grabbed a fistful of tissues. For a good thirty seconds, the two men, Mossmuss and Cribb, watched Dare sneeze and blow, blow and sneeze, until the fit had passed and he sank back bleary eyed into the mass of blue monogrammed pillows.

"Ingratitude! That's what! Six years of my life I've spent raising that little freak, that little *science experiment*. Six years I've put up with him bolting around the lab like Kid Flash. Dude! I had to harden every electronic device on the compound so he wouldn't fry the computers every time he pitched a fit. I put clothes on him. Good clothes, too! Stussy, Quiksilver — that kid was in *brands*. I fed him. I even read him bedtime stories. I frickin' hate bedtime stories. I even tucked him in! You guys saw it. More than once. Did you ever see my dad read *me* bedtime stories, Cribb?"

"No, sir."

"Did you ever see my dad tuck *me* in, Mossmuss?"

"I didn't see it."

"That's because he didn't! That's why." He put on a fake Welsh accent, mocking his dead father: "'No respectable father reads bedtimes stories. It's just not done. A child should be seen and not heard.' But, nooo! That's not how I played it. I was like one of those super-modern buddy dads. Maybe I overdid it. Letting him watch all that *Shining Time Station* crap. Now look at him. He just up and runs away. Drags me through the Two-Hearted Forest, through the snow and ice, gets me sick. And he takes the one thing I need the most. It's the only thing I really needed him for. Man, I tell you, if I…I…*Ahchoo!*"

Dare fell into another fit of sneezing. Cribb and Mossmuss exchanged weary glances. Dare took a pull of his inhaler and blinked his bleary eyes. "What was I saying? Yeah, right. When I get that kid back, I'm going to teach him what it means to be a Dare. He thinks I'm mean, some kind of bully? He hasn't seen anything yet."

"You wanted to see us?" said Mossmuss.

"I called you for a report," croaked Dare as he sank back into the pillows and massaged his temples.

"We'll be dockin' in Algiers by sun-up," said Cribb.

"And Chul?"

"He's still there, all right. Doing what we can't tell."

"This is odd," said Dare, still rubbing his temples. "I thought he'd try to make his way back to the Two-Hearted Forest."

"He's not alone, sir," said Mossmuss. "He's with a girl. One of our informants spotted them this evening in the Bab El Oued."

"A *girl*?"

"I'd lay down a hundred quid it's the same girl what was wit'im last night," said Cribb. "The one who plinched him out of the Two-Hearted

Forest."

"Plinching," spat Dare and winced. "One of the parlor tricks of the old families. I bet Georges Aminou thinks he's put one over on me. It's only so long that he can hide behind that weak old science. But I'll find him. And when I do, dude! I'll uproot dear old Mom right before his eyes."

"We got us a wood chipper wit'er name on it," said Cribb.

Dare spread a grin of small, fluorescent teeth. "Nice. I'll have some fun putting an end to the *Great Aminou Family*." He punctuated the last three words in air quotes. "And as for the girl. Anita, is that her name? What could she be doing in Algiers? Could Georges and Maryann be so dumb that they would send her off again? Alone?"

"She and Chul were seen by the same informant," said Mossmuss, "entering an electronics store owned by..." He looked down at the new science touch tablet in his hand, the kind modern people use to send letters instead of posting them by horse or pigeon. "... a Mohamed Kateb."

"Kateb!" Dare heaved forward and fell into a fit of sneezing and coughing and then something in between…snoughing…ceezing? He flailed for his inhaler and took a deep pull. When he could speak again, he was fairly seething. "Mo Kateb!"

"Whos'he?" asked Cribb.

"Mohammed Kateb is a repairer of magical devices—one of those broken-down *old science* professions. He may be the last one, I don't know. Although I hear he's been teaching his son the tricks of the trade, for whatever it's worth. Anyway, all of the old families know about him. They all go to him to fix this or tell them how to work that…" Dare took another pull of the inhaler. "What happened then?"

"What happened when?" said Cribb.

"When the kids visited Kateb!"

"We don't know," said Mossmuss. "Kateb cast a spell after Chul and the girl entered the store. Our man couldn't see what was going on. All's we know is that the girl and Chul left the store a few minutes later, empty handed."

"I don't like it. Not one bit. We'll have to pay Kateb a visit of our own, find out what he told them. But first, I want those kids on this ship. As soon as we arrive tomorrow, I want you two to go and get them and bring them back here. And no more of that plinching crap. This time, we'll be ready for their stupid magic tricks. And what with that girl as bait, I will be sure to draw out Georges and Maryann Aminou. Why," Dare sniffed, "this may just turn out better than I thought."

"What about the boy?"

"No harm can come to him. He's useless to me harmed. I want him and the thing he is carrying back here on this ship. Unscathed."

Mossmuss asked, "Do you mean that *car coo-coo* thing he stole?"

"It's pronounced *Kar-Chuh-LEW*, dimwit. And yes, it's a bit of the old science that I very much must have. It took me years to get that one, and I will not have it taken from me. My plans will be ruined if I don't have it—and Chul Sun—back here on this rust bucket."

"What good is it? If you don't mind us askin'," said Cribb.

"I *do* mind you asking, but I suppose I should explain. You two at least will need to be privy to my plans." Dare wiped his nose and threw a tissue toward the garbage can. Again, it missed by a wide margin. "What it is is a key. A key that will unlock a certain place that has lain hidden for the last six years. A certain place hidden under the rolling, green hills of Palo Alto, California."

Mossmuss leaned forward hungrily. "You mean the laboratory? The boy's parents' laboratory?"

"Bingo!" replied Dare. "Yes, in that lab is the secret of how they created that boy, how they unleashed the full potential of the human body. And once I have that secret, then, well, I'll put an end to the war between the old and new sciences once and for all. Those old families insulted my great-granddad Kelnick Dare, they mocked him and the new science. But look around you. The new science is surpassing the old everywhere you look. Once I have the secrets in that lab, the new science will finally bury the old science — and with it the last of the magical families."

"How ar'ya goin' to do that?" asked Cribb.

"How?" replied Dare, incredulous. "Think about it! Chul's parents made just him. Just one! Why stop at one dumb kid? Why not create a whole army of super-powered children to do my bidding? I will, of course, make them less willful than Chul Sun, less clever, more compliant, and much more bloodthirsty, ready to do anything I tell them. Dude! With an army like that, I'll be able to wipe all those old families off the map. I will avenge my great-granddad once and for all. And why stop there? With my army of super-Chuls, the nations will kneel before me. I'll rule the world!"

Dare's eyes had gained a dark luster, his breath smoothed by the adrenaline rush of all the gruesome possibilities that the *khar chuluu* opened before him. He gave a brief, pleasant shiver. "Yes, it will be awesome to walk right into that boy's parents' laboratory after all these years, and there will be nothing to stop me. No secret will be beyond my grasp."

"But how will y'do it?" asked Cribb. "How's that *char koo-doo* gonna get you in that lab when you've been lookin' all these years without no luck?"

"*Khar chuluu*, bird brain. And as for *how* it will help me get in there, that's for me to know and you to find out. Until then, I want those kids on this ship by nine o'clock tomorrow morning, and the *khar chuluu* with them. Understood?"

"Yes," croaked Cribb and Mossmuss in unison.

"Now, get out of here. And turn off the lights. All this talking to you numbskulls has given me a splitting headache."

Chapter 7

*In which Cribb and Mossmuss close
in, and we learn just how Chul Sun
came to possess the infamous*
khar chuluu.

The next morning, *subh sadiq*, true dawn,
stretched its arms across the breadth of the
sky, one hand out to sea, the other across
the cluttered skyline of Algiers, deep into the still
cool and mist-woven expanse of the desert. At
this groggy hour, just as the muezzin was
climbing the minaret of the grand mosque, two
strangers hoisted themselves up the seawall in
Algiers Harbor and stepped onto Rue d'Angkor
like they owned the place.

One man was large and wide with a plodding,

straight-ahead way of walking; the other was small and quick, with stuttery steps left and right. With my considerable eye I watched them. These were Dare's henchmen—Mossmuss and Cribb—looking something like a speedboat tacking back and forth alongside a slow-moving freighter. They made their way before the fish stalls and morning cafes of the harbor, in search of Anita the Reckless and the boy Chul Sun.

Mossmuss, the larger of the two, pulled a thin, black tablet out of his coat pocket and glanced at it. This was the same new science gizmo that he used to receive messages from Dare's informants. He teased out its secrets by poking at it and running his finger across its glossy surface. A map appeared and Mossmuss stopped to take his bearings while Cribb fidgeted anxiously. "Turn here," said Mossmuss, and they crossed the road and plunged away from the waterfront and into the heart of the Casbah.

"What if we don't find 'em?" asked Cribb, who continued his nervous tacking back and forth. "I mean, what if it don't work?"

"It'll work," said Mossmuss. "We tracked them all the way here from the Two-Hearted Forest. We'll get them this time."

"What was it the kid was looking for in the Two-Hearted Forest anyway?" asked Cribb. "I mean, what's there exceptin' a lot of trees and snow?"

Mossmuss eyed up Cribb. "Don't you start asking a lot of questions."

"Isn't you even curious about why he was there? Why wouldn't he go to Disneyland or something like that? Some place fun?"

Mossmuss said nothing, just stared at the tablet in his hand.

"You know, don't you?" asked Cribb. "Is'at why you ain't saying nothing? What's in the Two-Hearted Forest? Some kind of treasure? Some hidden gateway to an enchanted land?"

"A what?"

"A hidden gateway to an enchanted —"

"Shut it. It ain't nothing like that."

"Ah ha! So you do know! I knew it. Tell me. What it is?"

"I've been told by Dare not to tell anybody. Not even you."

"No need," said Cribb. "You don't need to tell me. Just think it. Picture it in your mind." He reached out and put his hand against the side of Mossmuss' face.

"What on earth are you doing?"

"A mind meld, mate. I'm gonna read your thoughts. Now hold still." Cribb's head lolled to the side and his eyes rolled back. "Ooohm! Ooohm! Mind reading in progress. Downloading...your file will be ready in twenty seconds..."

Mossmuss swatted Cribb away. "You're off your rocker!"

"Hey! I wasn't finished!"

Mossmuss brandished a massive fist. "Believe me, you're finished." He consulted the tablet. "OK, now, we're not far from those two kids. Now, you remember what to do, right? We'll only have one chance at this. We have to surprise them before that girl can plinch and Chul can jump into super speed. So we have to get the net over them before they see us."

Cribb reached into a satchel he was carrying at his side and pulled out the corner of a mesh net, its threads fine and shimmering like gossamer. "As if some flimsy fishing net's gonna keep 'em in."

"It's not just some fishing net, you loon. It cancels out their powers. That's the whole point. That's why we have to get it over them as fast as possible and when they're not expecting it. Once they're in the net, they'll be limp as ragdolls. I'll carry the boy, you carry the girl, and we we'll be back at the ship ricky-ticky."

"What're they doin' now?" asked Cribb.

"According to this, they're in an alley not far from here. Laying side by side. Looks like they're sleeping. So get your net ready."

Cribb let it unravel at his side. Then, drawing it up with the practiced hand of a fisherman, he gripped one end tightly and the other with loose fingers, ready to fling it over the unsuspecting children. "Now let's hope these guppies is truly sleeping. If so, this'll be easy fishing, no doubt about it."

With Mossmuss' great bulk leading the way, Cribb creeping behind, net dangling at his hip, they moved through the early morning streets of the Casbah, closing in on their quarry.

But the two children were not asleep. They were only pretending to be.

For a long time, one had been, indeed: For most of the night, Chul slept coiled in a ball on the magic carpet in an alleyway behind a metal dumpster, his body worn out following his long run across the desert the day before. Anita slept for a little while as well. She curled up next to Chul while I (the mighty Djinn of All Deserts!) was reduced to guarding the entrance to the alleyway like some mangy mutt. At her command, I had taken the form of an old man and groused at passersby, warding them away from the sleeping children.

Eventually, Anita woke up. It was perhaps an hour before *subh sadiq* and the arrival of Cribb and Mossmuss at the seawall in Algiers Harbor.

"Where are they now, oh mighty djinn?" Anita asked.

"Where are who?" I asked, though I knew who she was talking about. I am troublesome out of habit.

"Dare and his men," she said.

"Still sailing," said I. "But not far. They soon will be in Algiers harbor."

"And what about her?"

"Who?"

"My mother!"

"She has left your Aunt Tanya in Chicago and now I sense her here in Algiers. Getting closer. My goodness. She's plinched all over the known world in a single night looking for you, Anita the

Reckless. I hate to think what will happen when she finds you."

"She still can't see me, is that right, mighty djinn?"

"Of course not, master, as long as I am by your side. Or shall I show you to her so you can be on your way home? I can't hide you from Dare's new science. You know this. Once he finds you, unlike your mother, he will show you no mercy."

Anita the Reckless paid no heed to my sage words. I had said the same thing a hundred times that night, and I knew, though she would not admit it, that a hundred times that night she had been on the verge of plinching back to the house and being done with this foolishness. But a thought kept troubling her, something she felt she must pursue.

"Mighty djinn, can I ask you something?"

"Can I stop you?"

"Dare told Chul that the *khar chuluu* is a key. Why would he say something like that? The *khar chuluu* allows one person to become another person, right? How could it be used as a key?"

"Riddles are not my strong suit, master," said I. "You will have to ask Dare when he captures you."

"He's not going to capture me," she said. She turned and gave Chul a shove. "Wake up. C'mon, get up."

"Hm, huh? Where am I?"

"Sleeping in an alleyway in Algiers, where else? C'mon, get up, we need to talk."

When he was up and they had had a chance to eat some snacks from Anita's backpack, they sat with their backs to the brick wall. "Tell me," she said, "how did you get the *khar chuluu*?"

"I don't want to say."

"Look, if we are going to stop Dare, you need to tell me everything you know. Now, please tell me how you got it."

Chul crossed his arms in shame and hesitated. "I stole it."

"You *stole* it?"

"Yes. But I didn't want to. He made me."

"Where did you steal it from?"

"From a castle, I guess you can say it's a castle, on the Baltic Sea. A very old place that sits on a cliff, and it's made out of stone and has high walls all around it. Dare had planned this robbery for a long time, and he told me about it a lot, but he would never tell me what I was supposed to steal. He only told me that it was a very special thing.

An important thing. It was going to be my hardest robbery yet, he said, because the castle was protected by the old science, and there were still secrets of the old science that he had not yet figured out how to defeat. But for this crime, we were going to use stealth and cunning.

"The person that lives in the castle, I learned, is a man named Kristjan Tormis. Tormis spends nearly every moment in the castle alone, working on his books and writings. His family, what is left of it, lives in separate rooms and never sees the man except when he comes out Sundays to go to church in a chapel in the castle. A priest from the local parish comes up the long, steep stairway every Sunday to do church service. But the priest is never invited for coffee or tea. He's just sent back out by the service entrance when chapel is over.

"That is life in this castle, week after week, year after year. There is nothing motorized except for a few appliances in the kitchen run by a generator. At night, they say, the hallways are lit by oil lamps and the rooms warmed by fires that burn in the hearth places, but people say no smoke comes out of the chimneys. Some people in the village believe that the castle is haunted.

"Dare's spies had tracked the comings and goings of the vendors and shop keepers that brought deliveries of food and supplies to the castle. The delivery people are scared of the place and only a few will go in. When they do, they leave the deliveries in a hallway near the kitchen. The servants who live in the castle don't talk much to the people bringing food and supplies. They won't say anything about the mysterious family that lives there. And if you ask too many questions, you're told not to return.

"Somewhere in this castle was the thing that Dare wanted. He was not sure in what room it would be. He'd narrowed the possibilities down to three places: an old armory in the castle dungeon, a reliquary behind the alter in the chapel, or the library of Kristjan Tormis, the place where he did all of his work. To get into the castle I would need to be asked to come in. The castle is protected by an enchantment. Anyone who tries to enter without being invited is filled with a fear so bad they run away. I guess that's why people think it's haunted. The plan was for me to pose as a delivery boy and come in through the pantry. The staff had never seen me before and almost did not let me in, but I explained in Estonian that

I was new to the village and working for the grocer. I knew the language because I had been learning with a tutor for the last two years. That's how long Dare had planned this robbery. When the staff heard my fluent speech, they assumed I was telling the truth and let me in. I helped unload boxes and supplies into the pantry.

"The next goal was to draw Tormis from the library. We could only do this by tricking him. I got out a box cutter like I was going to cut some string and, as though by accident, I sliced open the palm of my hand. It hurt like crazy. It was really hard to do on purpose. But it would've been a lot worse for me with Dare if I failed. So I cut my hand open. And pretty bad. There was blood everywhere.

"Dare knew that the old codes required the head of household to render aid to an injured guest. Tormis, sensing trouble in the house, came out of his library to see what was happening. The servants took me into the kitchen where he met me. He was a kindly man, gentle, and really old. He sent the servants away and asked me to put my hand in his so he could look at it. He looked at it for a second and then ran the tip of his finger along the wound while saying an incantation.

The cut healed where he touched it. It was like a miracle, and I said so. He just shook his head. No, he said, it is no miracle, just the old science. There are some, he said, that still know how to use it. He smiled at me kindly. I was sorry to do what I did next, but I was more afraid of Dare than I was of doing something wrong.

"Just as Tormis was smiling at me, I went into super speed and, before he could react, I took out a punch syringe and injected a drug into his arm. He immediately fell over, unconscious. What Dare had created was not just a drug to make Tormis fall asleep. The drug also took away all of his powers. Dare guessed, and rightly it turns out, that it was the old man's powers that were protecting the house. That was the reason he could never leave.

"Still in super speed, I went from room to room looking for this thing that Dare had sent me to steal. The black stone, the *khar chuluu*. For me, when I am in super speed, it is like every hour that passes for me is a second for everyone else. For hours—of my time—I wandered from room to room of this great old castle above the sea. Everything was dead silent. The waves below were bundled up in mid-crash, the sea foam floating in mid-air. The sun stayed in the same place; the shadows did not move; the second hand on the clock stood motionless. The servants in the pantry looked like statues. It was an endless afternoon. I searched for a long time and finally found it. Like Dare had guessed, it was in Tormis' library, in the bottom drawer of the desk where he did all of his work.

"What happened next is hard to explain. When I touched the *khar chuluu*, I felt something. I could feel this, I don't know, power coming from it. It didn't come from Tormis or any person but from the thing itself. It was like, like a darkness coming out of it. It was like a warning. Though I had stolen a lot of things for Dare in super speed — money, jewels, weapons — I had never wanted to do any of it, but he would hurt me if I didn't and I didn't have anywhere else to go. But now, when I held this thing in my hand and felt this power coming out of it, I felt like if I took it back to him something bad would happen, something *very* bad. I knew I could never let Dare have it. So I decided right then to run away."

To hear this boy, Chul Sun, tell this story, drew me, the Djinn of All Deserts, away from the entrance of the alley to the place where he and

Anita were huddled behind the dumpster. The look on Anita's face echoed the amazement that I felt: Kristjan Tormis was the head of one of the four remaining old families. He was reputed to be one of the most powerful practitioners of the old science in the world, and this boy—this Chul Sun—had been able to rob him of one of his most highly protected possessions. It must have been true, then, what the magical people had been saying all these years, that the old science was dying. The old families could no longer safeguard their secrets or their way of life.

"So what did you do?" asked Anita. "How did you run away?"

"Well, I just put the *khar chuluu* into my pocket and walked out of there. I went out through the pantry, where Tormis was still on the floor frozen in time, and followed the path down to the sea. In super speed, the surface of water is like concrete, cold and dimpled, and you can walk right on it. I climbed up and down over the frozen waves all the way across the Baltic until I reached Tallinn. By that time, I had been in super speed for nearly six hours of my time—six seconds to the rest of the world—and I was exhausted. I returned to normal speed and the world returned around me with a whoosh: the noise of the cars and the trains and the people. It was cold. Snow drifted down from the sky. The church bells chimed two p.m.

"I was too tired to return to super speed, but I knew I could not stop. In a few minutes, Dare would know that something was wrong and he and Cribb and Mossmuss, his guys, would come after me. I checked my position by the sun and began walking south, toward the Two-Hearted Forest."

"Why the Two-Hearted Forest?" asked Anita. "Why did you go there?"

"It's hard to explain. Promise not to laugh?"

"Only if it's not funny."

"Seriously," said Chul.

"OK, seriously. I won't laugh."

"Well, it's like this. At first, Dare told me that I was his son, right? Later, he admitted that I wasn't his son, not for real, but that he had adopted me after my parents had died. He told me that no one else wanted me, because of my powers.

"But for a long time, I've had this strange feeling. I've had this feeling that even this was not true. I have this memory. Or maybe it's a dream. I have this memory of a woman. The woman looks just like me. I mean, she's Korean like me, and I am looking up at her face, and she is the most beautiful woman that I have ever seen. And in this memory—or this dream, or whatever it is—she is looking at me and saying, 'Remember the Two-Hearted Forest.' She says this over and over. 'Remember the Two-Hearted Forest.'"

"What else does she say?"

"That's it," said Chul. "That's all she says. Just 'Remember the Two-Hearted Forest.' Of course, I had no idea what that might mean for a long time until one day I was in the study of the house where Dare keeps all of his father's old books. I was looking through an atlas when I noticed that one of the pages was taken out. It was the page that showed Eastern Europe. I thought that was strange, so I looked at another one of his atlases and I found a page torn out there too. In the same place, in Eastern Europe. Dare's father had lots of atlases, you see. He liked to collect books. And every one that I looked at, it was the same thing. That page was missing."

"So what did it mean?"

"I didn't know. I mean, I made no connection

between the missing pages and the Two-Hearted Forest at first, but then one time Dare was out of the country. Doing something bad, no doubt. And like I always do, I went into the study to read his father's books and go through his old things. Well, there was a certain desk in the study that Dare always kept locked and I had never been able to get into. But lately, I had been reading books about picking locks — there were lots of books about picking locks — and I was getting pretty good at it. So I decided to try to pick the lock in the desk in the study. It was not easy. In fact, it was harder to pick than any other lock I had encountered, so I decided that there must be something very interesting in there. I stayed up all night, all the next day, and most of the next night until I finally got it. I opened it. And when I opened it, I found all of the missing pages to the atlases. All of them. And on each one, I found the same thing: the Two-Hearted Forest. Sometimes in English. Sometimes in French, German, Latin, Russian, Romanian, Hungarian. All of these different maps, dating back centuries, all had the Two-Hearted Forest written on them.

"I was amazed. It couldn't have been a coincidence, right? Me having these dreams or memories or whatever they were and the fact that Dare had tried to hide the existence of the Two-Hearted Forest from me. Well, just then, Dare arrived home—earlier than expected. I tried to relock the desk, but I found that once picked, it could not be relocked. Dare came into the house. When he found the desk unlocked, well…"

"What did he do?"

"I'd rather not say. It was bad. The worst punishment I ever got."

"And why didn't you just jump into super speed to get away from him? Or shock him with your pulse?"

"He knows how to defeat my powers. He can use the new science to make me weak as a normal boy. That's how he was able to beat Kristjan Tormis. That is how he'll be able to beat your parents too if he finds them. That's why I had to get away. I knew after that beating that Dare would kill me once he was done using me. He even said as much. That day I stole the *khar chuluu* from Tormis I had this feeling that somehow my usefulness to Dare was coming to an end. So I took the *khar chuluu* and I headed straight for the Two-Hearted Forest. And here's the really crazy part. Do you really promise not to laugh?"

"Cross my heart."

"That woman, Anita. I think that woman was my mother. I think that, somehow, she was trying to tell me something. I felt somehow that she was calling me from beyond the grave."

To all this, even I, the Djinn of All Deserts, was listening with rapt attention. Normally, I could not care less about the comings and goings of human beings, but as I listened, I actually felt the pang of something quite unusual—curiosity. I found myself reaching out with my considerable eye to the Two-Hearted Forest, but I could not find the woman, this boy's mother. If she was there, she was hidden from my sight by the strong new science. And then I felt something else too. For the first time in thousands of years I felt—just a little—fear. "This Dare," said I, "will he even destroy the djinn?"

"My parents say that Dare wants to destroy all of the old science," she answered. "All of the spells and spirits of old Earth and of the old science will disappear forever. Magic will be nothing more than entertainment for children. That is why Dare's great-grandfather Kelnick broke away from the five families. He decided that the new science would eventually win out over the old science. He guessed that the great houses would eventually be nothing more than feeble old men and families hiding in the desert. I guess he was right."

"We have to stop him," said Chul.

"Ah, but you have two more immediate problems," said I.

"What's that?" asked Anita.

True dawn had stretched its roseate fingers across the sky, while across the city the interlaced voices of the muezzins echoed, calling the city to prayers. It was at that moment that I saw Dare's henchmen climbing onto the quay at Algiers Harbor.

"Two men," said I. "Cribb and Mossmuss have just arrived in Algiers and they are on their way here at this moment. And if that isn't enough, Anita the Reckless, your mother has just left Mo's Electronics and is headed in this direction. Cribb and Mossmuss from the east; Mother Maryann from the west. That puts you two in between. Now, I wonder, how will you get yourself out of this predicament?"

"We're going to plinch out of here," said Anita. "And you're coming with us. But first, I have a plan."

Chapter 8

*In which Anita, Chul, and the Djinn
of All Deserts outfox Cribb and
Mossmuss, and in which Chul
begins to unlock the mystery of
the* khar chuluu.

"All right," said Mossmuss to Cribb. "This here's almost the place." He was looking down at the black tablet in his hand, upon which was fixed the location of Anita and Chul. In the minutes since the two men had arrived in Algiers, the children had settled down side-by-side, as if still sleeping. Mossmuss' tablet showed two motionless blips. He could not see me—the Djinn of All Deserts—because his new science gadget was designed to detect humans, not beings, like me, made from smokeless fire. They crept closer, guided by the light of the touch pad.

"Now get ready with that net," whispered Mossmuss. "We'll only get one chance to get it over them. If Chul wakes up before you cast, he'll run right out of there fast as lightning."

Cribb nodded gravely and gripped the gossamer net, his muscles tight and ready. He followed closely at Mossmuss' shoulder as they rounded the corner into the alley where they expected to find Anita and Chul sleeping.

"What?" said Mossmuss, stopping short. "Who are you?"

Standing before them was a withered old man in a tattered robe blocking their way into the alley. The feet of Anita and Chul could be seen splayed motionless on the far side of a metal dumpster.

The man put out his hand. "Alms for the poor?"

"We ain't got no alms for the poor," spat Cribb. "Now get out of the way."

The old man did not move. "Please, sirs, a few coins would be fine. Anything."

Mossmuss tried to go around, but the old man

stepped in front of him. "Please, sirs."

"You best get out of the way, old man," snarled Mossmuss. "We got business here."

The old man did not look flustered in the least. "A bit of bread? No? How about the air in your head?"

With that, Mossmuss cocked his arm and took a swing at the old man, but instead of striking him, his fist went straight through as if he had punched so much loose, dry sand.

The old man looked down calmly at Mossmuss' arm stuck through his chest. "How rude! You should never hit THE DJINN OF ALL DESERTS!" The old man, of course, was I, the all-seeing-one, who had watched the two dullards approaching the alley as you might two toddlers playing hide-and-seek. With a twirl of my wrist, I whipped myself into a vortex of wind and sand that blew away the trash and whirled Cribb and Mossmuss into the alleyway.

"Now!" yelled Anita.

She and Chul leaped to their feet. She plunged headlong into the sandstorm and, finding Mossmuss, locked her arms around the gigantic man. He was so big she had to climb up his back and wrap her arms around the tops of his shoulders. Clasping her fingers in front of him, she locked him in an embrace from which he could not escape. Chul, meanwhile, jumped into super speed and, winding his way through the sand suspended all around him, found Cribb mid-stagger, one foot up, the other pinioned on the heel of his boot. Chul delicately plucked the gossamer net from Cribb's fingers and flashed away, so that by the time Cribb's foot hit the ground, the net was gone.

Cribb held up his empty hands. "Uh oh, mate."

Just then, Anita released the enormous Mossmuss. Using her telekinetic powers, she shoved the big man toward his cohort. Mossmuss fell over Cribb in a shower of obscenities, and then the two looked up in horror to see Chul leaping over them with the gossamer net. Underneath, they found themselves as weak as babies, not even able to lift a finger in their own defense.

I, the Djinn of All Deserts, meanwhile, had retaken the shape of a flicker of desert heat. I must admit the sight of the two goons writhing helplessly left me with a twinkle of pleasure. "Master," said I at Anita's heel. "Your mother is coming!"

"Quick," she said to Chul, "we need to get out of here."

He hoisted her into his arms and bolted straight up the side of the building, I following like a shimmer of heat rising from a flame. When we reached the top of the building, Chul set Anita behind the low roof wall, from which they could peer stealthily down at the street below.

A stately woman in a marigold dress and matching handbag came walking briskly down the sidewalk. Her posture and gait exuded confidence, but her face was riven with concern. Not far from the alleyway, she stopped and, putting her hands out to her sides, turned in a slow circle, as if taking a deep breath of the morning air. Lost in concentration in some inward world, she took no notice of the Casbah locals staring at her quizzically.

"Who's that?" asked Chul. "She's so beautiful!" Her skin was deep brown and smooth, her hair sculpted and brightly black against the golden yellow of her dress. She was too pretty for the rough streets around her but, then again, somehow perfectly comfortable. She looked like a woman who knew how to take care of herself and a dozen other people to boot.

"That's my mom," whispered Anita.

"How did she find us?"

"She hasn't. The djinn is hiding us from her. She's here because Mo Kateb told on us. To save his own butt, no doubt. I should have known that the guy would run off and tell my parents. She can't sense us through the spell cast by the djinn, but she can still see us if she looks up. So we have to stay down."

Chul and Anita watched as Maryann Aminou turned in a circle, searching for them with her inner eye. She probed the air around them, but I, the Djinn of All Deserts, scattered her senses like a flock of pigeons. I did not conceal from her inner sight, however, the two men lying helpless in the alley below. She felt their presence immediately — all black denim and greasy teeth. Opening her eyes, she stepped forward cautiously and, peering around the corner into the alley, found Mossmuss and Cribb paralyzed beneath the gossamer threads of the incapacitation net. She recognized at once that Thorium Dare's handiwork had been turned against them. They looked up at her, helpless, humiliated, yet, she could tell, relieved that she had been the one to find them in this predicament and not their master.

"So, well, Mum," said Cribb, trying on a grimy smile, "you think you could help us?"

"Where did they go?" she asked, her arms crossed, her expression unimpressed.

"Where did who go?" asked Mossmuss thickly.

"The children."

He did not dare to admit that they had been outfoxed by two kids but merely let his eyes trace the steep ascent up the brick wall to the top of the building. Maryann immediately plinched to the roof. When she got there, Anita and Chul were gone.

At that moment, three thousand kilometers away, Anita, Chul and I, the Djinn of All Deserts, piled out of a plinch point into the Aminou cabin deep in the Two-Hearted Forest. The cabin was still a wreck from Anita and Chul's quarrel two nights before. Books and bedding, butter and andirons lay scattered across the floor of the once-cozy cabin. A mattress was slumped beside the toppled sideboard. The rocking chair lay on its side, one rocker snapped clean off. The door leaned against the wall where it had been blown off its hinges by Dare. Bright winter light poured in. And it was cold. Very cold. Chul immediately missed the balmy air of Algiers. Even I gave a shiver—and I'm made of smokeless fire. "How can people live here in the detestable north?"

Anita, exhausted from her second transcontinental plinching in two days, sat back against the wall. It was all she could do to conjure a fire in the hearth before falling fast asleep. I had returned to the shape of an old man and squatted by the fire while Chul leaned the door upon its hinges, trying to block out a little of the cold.

That being done, he circled the room picking up things and filling his pockets: a frozen hank of bread, a scarf, an extra pair of socks.

I watched him. "What are you doing?"

"I'm leaving," he said. "I've put Anita in enough danger."

I could not help but snort at the comedy of that. "Little good that will do now."

"What do you mean?"

"That girl has put *herself* in danger. When she enslaved me and went to Algiers out of the protection of her parents. Had she wanted to be safe, she would have stayed at home. Have you thought of that?"

"No, not really," said Chul.

"That man she seeks, that you ran away from, Thorium Dare, he was a danger to the Aminou family before he was a danger to you. He's a danger to me now. To all of us."

"I didn't ask for her help."

"I don't see how that is the point," said I. "Look, I am a djinn and we djinn do not often meddle in the affairs of humans, but you are not my master, she is, and I will tell you that I have seen many masters come and go. Many mighty and powerful men and women, and almost to a person they have destroyed themselves. There is one thing that has bound them all: pride. Pride to think that they could control all magic by themselves, pride to think that they didn't need anybody else's help to survive. Trust me when I say, you cannot escape from Thorium Dare by yourself, and she cannot defeat him by herself. If you leave now, you will be putting her in greater danger and yourself too. Do you not see this?"

"You *are* a troublesome djinn," said Chul.

I smiled despite myself — I, the Djinn of All Deserts, actually smiled. "Pfah," said I, "I am just an old spirit bound to a thousand masters. A slave forever." At this, my smile disappeared.

"What is the point of all of my mighty powers when I must live forever in the thrall of a thousand feckless humans?"

"Is there any way you can be free?" asked Chul.

"There is a way," said I after some hesitation. "But it is nothing I may speak of, and it has yet to happen in all my thousands of years living in the service of humans. So I can foresee no change in my condition. But then again, I see no change in yours either. You humans, I mean. I have watched you all for millennia. You are not free, though you may think you are. But unlike the me, you humans may choose your master. Many of you are slaves to your pride, to your hatred, your lusts and fears—these are the people like Thorium Dare. There are others, a precious few, who choose a different path. They choose a master greater than themselves and their petty desires. They live for a deeper purpose. And there are others, a great many in between, who struggle all their days in their hearts between one side and the other."

"And what about Anita?"

I watched the girl sleeping and thought about this. "This one," said I, "is struggling in her heart.

She came to me because she wanted to prove herself to her parents and her ancestors. She wanted to prove that she could find and defeat Thorium Dare. It was pride that drove her. I could see this as clearly as I can see you in front of me. But pride is not enough to defeat a man like that."

"What do you know about Dare?" asked Chul Sun.

"I know that he is powerful enough to hide something from my sight. He doesn't bother to hide himself, but there is something more important to him, something he desperately wants to keep hidden, at least until the right time. I don't know what this thing may be, but I sense, based on everything that you have said, that it is very near to where we are."

"Can you see anyone? With your powers?"

"Mostly, if I choose to. But this new science can hide things from my sight. It blocks my vision."

"Can you see my mom and dad?" asked Chul, hopefully.

Once again, I looked for them. I cast my considerable eye across the Two-Hearted Forest. I looked farther afield. I looked across oceans and deserts. I looked into cities and towns. On the water and beyond the water. I searched kitchens, sleeping chambers, hallways, ball rooms, and rooftop gardens. I searched barrios, tenements, glitzy boulevards, and the outskirts of ten thousand cities. I scoured night forests for them, prairies, mountaintops, caves and grottos, empty sunset beaches on the other side of the world. All of this I looked across as you might your bedroom.

"I cannot find them among the living," said I, "and I may not see what is beyond. That other place is for better beings: for God and the angels."

Chul sat back and watched the fire. Fingers of flame climbed the logs and fell back again, the flicker and whisper, the shifting heat, the tender tic, tic, tic of water loosening from wood, the ancient aroma of forest and smoke.

"Mighty djinn?" Chul asked.

"Yes?"

"Can Dare be defeated?"

"All humans can be defeated," said I. "You just have to know their weaknesses."

"What are his weaknesses?"

"You know that better than I do."

"The *khar chuluu*," said Chul.

"What about it?"

"Dare told me that it was a key. Why would he have told me that it was a key?"

"I can whip you up a sandstorm to smite your enemies, Chul Sun, or conjure a pool of quicksand, but I'm not much good at riddles."

Chul was pacing now, thinking hard. "How could something that can turn you into any living person be used as a key? And what would it be a key *to*?"

"Maybe he was lying?"

"No, he wasn't lying. No, you're right, mighty djinn, I do know his weaknesses. He can't help but show off. He always wants people to know how clever he is. He would not have said the *khar chuluu* is a key unless he meant it. So, if it is a key, then we just have to figure out what it is a key to. And does it, do you think, have something to do with the Two-Hearted Forest? Why would he have hidden all of those maps to the Two-Hearted Forest? Who was he hiding them from? There was just Cribb, Mossmuss, and me—" Chul stopped short. He went to the window and looked out onto the snow-blanketed forest under the bright blue sky. Everything everywhere was still as stone, just the occasional quiver of branch shadow on white.

"What?" said I. "What are you thinking of?"

Chul said, "She told me, 'Remember the Two-Hearted Forest.' Somehow, she knew. She must have known."

"OK, now I'm confused."

Chul knelt down next to where Anita was sleeping against the wall. "Wake up, Anita!"

"What, wha—" she said, groggily.

"Wake up. I need you to do something. I need you to use the *khar chuluu*!"

This woke her up indeed. "What? It's haram—forbidden. Besides, I don't know how to use it. Mo said the incantation so fast that I couldn't follow it. I wouldn't know what to say to make it work even if I wanted to."

Chul laughed mischievously and tapped his noggin. "I have it. You see, Dare taught me how to hear and remember things like that. I heard it perfectly even though Mo tried to say it so fast that we wouldn't understand. It's a simple incantation. It goes like this:

Khar chuluu, *I come to thee with a wish to be*
The body who touches this thing I see.

Khar chuluu, *I come to thee with a wish to be*
The mind who knows this thing I see.

Khar chuluu, *I come to thee with a wish to be*
The soul who loves this thing I see.

"Just that?" asked Anita. "In English?"

"I think it's the meaning that's important, not the words. Remember the power comes from the stone, not the magic of the person who uses it. The incantation must simply make sure that the stone understands exactly what the person holding it wants it to do."

Anita smiled. "Sounds like something from one of my dad's boring lectures on the theory of the old science."

"Now take out the *khar chuluu*," said Chul. "If I'm right about what Dare wants to do with that stone, this should work."

She reached into her pocket and removed the item. Remembering how Mo had conjured her father back in Algiers, she held the stone gingerly. "OK, who am I supposed to become with this?"

"My mother," said Chul. "I want you to become my mother."

Chapter 9

*In which Chul Sun talks to two people
in the same person at the same time,
and Anita the Brave hatches a plan
to find a secret prison.*

Anita watched Chul for a moment, her expression grave, full of doubt. "Are you sure you want me to try to become your mother?" she asked. "What if it doesn't work? What if, I mean...you know."

Chul thought about this. He searched down through his feelings. He was desperate to find his parents and terrified that he wouldn't. But his resolve was stronger than his fear. This was why he had come to the Two-Hearted Forest after fleeing the castle in Estonia. He had to continue down this path even if the truth turned out to be far more difficult than the journey. He said, "I need to know. I need to know whether my parents are truly dead. But, see, the thing is, if they are not dead, there is only one person in the world that can hide them from the Djinn of all Deserts. That is Dare."

Anita seemed about to reply, but then she did something quite unexpected. She did something that had never been done before in my thousands of years of servitude among humans. She turned to me, the Djinn of All Deserts, and asked, "What do you think?"

I was so taken aback I could barely muster a reply. "Are you asking my opinion, master?"

"Yes. Why not?"

Until that moment, I had been crouched by the fire in the shape of a churlish old man, but then came a change in me. I stood up and felt myself transform into the shape of a young man. I found myself smiling, *yet again*. Said I: "All of my life, humans have only commanded me. They only called me 'great' or 'mighty' because they wanted something from me, but never has any master come to me seeking my counsel. Anita the Brave, you have treated me with great respect."

"Yeah...so what do you think?" asked Anita.

"I think you should use it. The *khar chuluu* was banned because of the terrible things that those with wicked hearts could do with it. But in the hands of the virtuous, great power becomes great virtue. You have to try it, if only to find out whether what Chul the Swift says is true: that perhaps his mother and father are still alive."

"OK," said Anita. "We'll try it. But Mo said that we need something cherished by Chul's mother, something she loved and desired with the fullness of her spirit. What is that thing?"

Chul recalled the look on the face of the woman in the memory, or the dream, from when he was a child. The tears and pain in her eyes when she said *Remember the Two-Hearted Forest.* "That thing, I think—I hope—is me."

Anita understood. She nodded, and slowly, nervously, she took Chul by the hand. She looked into his eyes and, pressing the *khar chuluu* to her chest, she recited the words that he had told her:

Khar chuluu, *I come to thee with a wish to be*
The body who touches this thing I see.

Anita said these words slowly, clearly, to make her will known to the stone.

Khar chuluu, *I come to thee with a wish to be*
The mind who knows this thing I see.

The edges of the girl began to shimmer and bend like the ground under desert heat.

Khar chuluu, *I come to thee with a wish to be*
The soul who loves this thing I see.

And, just as had happened in Mo's shop, Chul watched in fear and fascination as, dreamlike, Anita's features began to shift and change. Taking shape in front of him, Chul saw the woman he had seen so many times in his dreams. She was thinner now, worn by time, suffering and worry. Her features where delicate, skin pale, with soft brown eyes and hair streaked through with gray lying flat against her shoulders. She wore a simple dress of dark blue against which her trembling, furrowed hands seemed to hover. He knew her instantly — the fall of her shoulders, the tilt of her head, her warmth, the way she smelled. He knew this in his heart, his mind, and his soul. It was his mother. She was truly alive! Not only that, but she loved him, truly loved him, with all of herself as only a mother or a father could love. When the change was complete, an expression of confusion passed across her face—and then of recognition. She held his hand more tightly. Love and fear mixed within Chul. He began to tremble. Tears came to his eyes. "Mommy?"

"Yes, baby," she said. She took him into her arms and held him. "It's me. It's me. It's me."

"But why?" he asked. "Where did you go?"

"To the Two-Hearted Forest, baby. Just like I told you. Oh, we've tried so many times to come back to you," she said. "But there was no way out. The prison he put us in was too strong. But we thought about you every single day, Chul. We prayed for you every night, sweet baby."

"Who?" asked Chul. "Who put you in prison? And where?"

"You know who. Thorium Dare. In the Two-Hearted Forest. He faked our deaths. He pretended to have us buried. He was the one who took you away from us."

"Why did he do that?"

She pulled herself away from him. She was

crying even harder now. "You have to forgive us, Chul, for what we did to you!"

"What *you* did to me?"

"Your powers. The speed. The electromagnetism. Your father and I, we were blinded by our ambition. We discovered how, through magneto-genetic manipulation, we could give human beings extraordinary powers. We had finally figured out how to use the new science to achieve the miracles of the old science. Our first experiment was you. You were to be our demonstration, our greatest achievement. But we should have never done it. If we had known what it would cost you, how you would suffer, we would never have done something like that."

"What do you mean?"

"What I mean, Chul, is that when Thorium Dare learned about you, he decided that he had to have you. His family has been trying for a century to use the new science to destroy the old science once and for all. He saw you as a perfect weapon against the old science. He came to take you. You don't remember. You were too little. We were in Patagonia together, hiking in the mountains, when they came for us. Your father and I tried to fight back, but he and his men were too strong. They took you. Your dad and I thought he was going to kill us at first. Instead, he imprisoned us. He demanded to know how we made you—how we gave you your powers. We refused, of course, but he would not take no for an answer. Oh, the things he did to us to get us to talk. Then, he demanded that we take him to our laboratory in Palo Alto, to show him how to get in. Again, we refused. He threatened us. He threatened you. But we knew that we could never allow him to have the technology that gave you your powers. If he had our secrets, then there would be no end to the horrible things he could do."

Chul's mother looked at the black stone she was holding in her hand.

"It was then that Dare became obsessed with this. The *khar chuluu*. He must have known. I mean, the legend has been around for a long time. Dare knew that if he had you alive and us alive, then he could use the *khar chuluu* to become one of us, really *become* one of us. He would know everything we know. He would know exactly where our laboratory is located, all of our passcodes, and he would be able to trick all of the bio scans. All of the protections that we set up around our laboratory would be useless. He could stroll right in."

Chul's mother said, "So that's why he said the *khar chuluu* was a key!"

"What?" said Chul, confused.

"Oh, sorry, hi, this is Anita," said Chul's mother. "I'm here too."

"Where?" asked Chul.

"Inside your mom. It's hard to explain. But I'm here and she's here. We're here together, but I can step in and take control whenever I want. That's the power of the *khar chuluu*. I know everything she knows. That is why Dare said that the *khar chuluu* is a key."

"Yes," said Chul's mother. "Hi, it's me, Mom again. Yes—it's like a key to our laboratory. It's a key to the place where we kept all of our secrets. I'm so sorry for what you've gone through, Chul. For what we've done to you."

"Don't be so hard on yourself," said his mother.

"What?" asked Chul.

"It's me, Anita, talking again. You can't be so hard on yourself. My parents gave me my powers, in a sense. They could have chosen not to."

"But, Anita, that is the way of the old science. Yours are powers that Dare cannot steal."

Chul said, "Wait, guys, you're confusing me. You both sound like my mother. Who's talking now?"

"Anita here. Hi. I was just saying that she can't be so hard on herself."

"Who?"

"Your mom. Me."

"What? Forget it," said Chul. "Just let me talk to my mom."

"I'm here."

"Where's Dad?"

"He's with me. He's safe, but he's sick. He's not doing well."

"Let me see him."

Chul's mother nodded — or Anita did, it was hard to tell. The *khar chuluu* was still in her hands. She recited the incantation and transformed into Chul's father. The man looked years older than his mother. He was stooped and nearly bald except for a few gray wisps matted to the top of his head. He squinted at his son through smudged spectacles.

"Chul? Chul, my boy, look how much you've grown. I...we...thought we would never see you again. I...did you see your mother?" He looked around. "What is this place?"

"We're in a cabin owned by the Aminous in the Two-Hearted Forest," said Chul.

The man smiled. "The Aminous. Well, there's a name I haven't heard in many years. How are Georges and Maryann? They're good. And is this...are you little Anita? Not so little now. I'm twelve years old. Wonderful, wonderful. What are you doing here? What is going on? Well, school was out for the winter break. I was at our house in Algeria when my dad sent me to the Two-Hearted Forest —"

"OK, guys, you're confusing me again."

"Yes, yes," said Chul's father, and he fell to coughing. "I...well, please, you should talk to your mother. I don't feel so good."

Again, Anita, from inside Chul's father, recited the incantation and Chul's mother returned.

She smiled at him. "So tell me what is going on. How did you get to this place?"

He told her the whole story about how Dare had sent him to steal the *khar chuluu* from Kristjan Tormis and how after he had stolen the object, he ran away to the Two-Hearted Forest where he met Anita. He told his mother about Anita's father's house in the desert, the Djinn of All Deserts (me!), Algiers, about how Cribb and Mossmuss had tried to capture them, how they tricked the men and were able to plinch back into the Two-Hearted Forest before being found by Maryann Aminou. Anita interrupted from time to time, correcting Chul or adding her two cents, so that it seemed to him after a while that he could sense the girl floating invisibly in the air and speaking through his mother like a medium. The *khar chuluu* was truly a strange and powerful thing.

When they were finished with their story, Chul's mother spoke again. "That was quite an adventure. You did the right thing running away from Dare, but you should have stayed with the Aminous. They would have kept you safe."

"I thought I would bring them more trouble. Trouble seems to follow me wherever I go."

"The Aminous are a brave family and good people. They are true masters of the old science. Virtuous masters, not like Thorium Dare's ancestors before they broke from the great houses. Dare has been looking for the Aminous' desert house for many years."

"Yes, but the most important thing now," said Chul, "is that we find you and Dad. You have to show us how to get to where you are."

Chul's mother smiled sadly and stroked his hair. "That's the problem. I don't know where we are exactly." She went to the window and Chul followed. Looking out, all he could see were dark tree trunks and naked branches etched against snow and sky. She said, "I only know that we are imprisoned somewhere out there in the Two-Hearted Forest.

"The day that Dare took you away from us, I overheard him talking to Mossmuss. Dare thought I was unconscious because he had drugged your dad and me when he kidnapped us. But I had come out of it when I heard him talking about bringing us here to the Two-Hearted Forest. That was all I knew. Later, he told us to say goodbye to you one last time. This was not kindness but cruelty. I think he liked to see us in so much pain. I took you in my arms and looked you in the eyes and said the only thing I could think of: "Remember the Two-Hearted Forest." Dare was furious. He took you away and promised that we would never see you again. For a long time, I wondered if it was a mistake, saying what I said to you, but then those words felt like a lifeline between you and me. I felt that somehow you would remember what I said and that you would somehow find your way back to us." She pressed tears from her eyes. "And here you are."

"I did remember," said Chul. "I remembered all the time. I thought it was a dream. You seemed like an angel to me. I didn't know it was really you." He put his arms around his mother and they held each other for a long time.

Finally, Anita broke in, speaking through Chul's mother. "Sorry, guys. I hate to interrupt, but we have to act fast. It won't be long until Dare realizes that Cribb and Mossmuss didn't catch us. He will come looking for us."

Chul had the creepy feeling he was now hugging Anita. He pulled away. "This is so weird."

"It's the *khar chuluu*," said Anita. "It's like I'm the captain of a ship. I can let go and let your mother be your mother, or I can take over and do what I want. Or anything in between. I can see everything she sees and feel everything she feels. I have all of her memories, her knowledge, everything."

Chul said, "With the *khar chuluu*, Dare could become my mom or dad, find the laboratory, get inside, and create more people like me."

"Exactly," said Chul's mother. "That is why it was important to keep us alive. Or just barely. It was necessary to keep you alive too, in order to complete the transformation."

"Mighty djinn," said Anita, "where is Thorium Dare now?"

"He is on an airplane headed this way. He doesn't look happy."

"And Cribb and Mossmuss?"

"They are with him."

"So she did what I thought she would," said Anita.

"Who did?" asked Chul.

"My mother. She let them go so they could go back to Dare and tell him we had escaped. My parents won't be far behind. We need to go before they find us here."

"I don't think that's a good idea," said Chul. "We can't take on Dare, Cribb, and Mossmuss without your parents."

"Who says we're going to do this without them?" said Anita. "But we don't have much time. We have to find the place where Dare is keeping your parents. And your mom and I—I guess, since I am inside her—are going to get us there. So grab your things and the magic carpet and let's go."

Chapter 10

*In which Anita the Brave and Chul
Sun trick Thorium Dare into leading
them to his hidden prison only to find
themselves in their worst
predicament yet.*

A single set of footprints was drawn like a
dotted line across the virgin crust of
snow, a lonely figure with her arms
folded across her chest, her shadow slipping and
snapping over the drifts and embankments that
rolled like dunes over the floor of the Two-
Hearted Forest. High above, Chul sat cross-
legged on the teal magic carpet, his back straight,
eyes focused on the figure plodding high kneed
through the drifts and banks. This was his first

experience in carpeted flight and he exulted in the bright warm sun and the rush of flight. The next moment, he glanced sideways and was seized by a fear of falling off and plunging fifty meters to the forest floor. I, the Djinn of All Deserts, had no need for such clumsy conveyances as a flying carpet, but I hung beside him in the form of a shard of heat and gave the boy periodic updates on the progress of Thorium Dare. "He's thirty kilometers away and closing in fast," said I. "He's in one of those whirling things that people ride in."

"A helicopter?"

"Yes, that's it. Silly thing."

Chul smiled. "We should keep low. We need to make sure that he sees my mom—or I guess I should say Anita—before he sees us. How are they doing down there?"

I cast my considerable eye to the side of Chul's mother, heaving over a snow-covered log, Anita riding along, the invisible captain inside her. "They are cold but otherwise fine," said I.

Chul tapped the carpet. "Carpet, down." It shuddered and dropped toward the tangle of treetops. "Easy. Easy! Up! Up!" The carpet pulled up again, and Chul had to hang on for dear life.

It didn't like to be grabbed like this and flipped all the way over so that for several terrifying seconds, Chul was dangling from the edges, his feet dragging along the topmost tree branches. "Flip, carpet. Flip!"

"Turn over before I cook you, you impudent rug!" said I. The carpet promptly complied and Chul climbed back aboard nervously.

"Thanks, Djinn of All Deserts."

"Don't mention it. There's a reason people stopped flying on these things. Fickle contraptions."

"Status on Dare?"

"Twenty-five kilometers."

"He'll see us here if we're not careful. OK, let's try this. Stop and hover, carpet. Down *slowly*." The carpet descended gently through the trees until we were suspended about three meters above where his mother's footprints cut through the snow. "Follow the footprints," he said. "Impulse speed."

"Impulse speed?"

"A Star Trek joke," said Chul. "Don't worry about it."

The carpet seemed to catch Chul's meaning, however, and the three of us—boy, djinn, and carpet — drifted slowly and steadily over snow-smoothed hills and gulches through the Two-Hearted Forest. After some time, we could hear the hum of the rotors. "Ten kilometers," said I. "I believe Dare has spotted your mother."

"Dude, easy!" groaned Dare, jostled unhappily by Mossmuss' clumsy piloting. The big man had had some helicopter training — just enough to scare the wits out of his passengers. The helicopter jittered and dropped closer to the treetops. "Bring it down easy, you idiot!" Something far ahead in a break in the trees caught his eye. "Wait! Who's that?"

Dare and Mossmuss spotted a lone figure making its way through the forest of winter-bare trees.

Cribb, seated behind, zoomed in close with a camera mounted on the nose of the chopper. "It's…what?…it looks like…Hyun-ju Sun."

"Chul's mum?" choked Mossmuss.

"It can't be!" growled Dare. "Let me see that!" He pulled Cribb back from the screen and looked. "It's a trick! I know it. Bring us down in her path. Whoever that is, she's testing my patience."

Mossmuss darted out in front of the figure,

circled, and brought the helo down into a clearing directly in her path. Dare, Mossmuss, and Cribb piled out. Dare was bundled in a heavy winter coat, thermal gloves, knee-high boots. Still he shivered. "Gad! I hate this place. I hate the cold." He stabbed a gloved finger at Mossmuss and Cribb. "Now, don't screw this up, you idiots. If she gets away, I'll have both your heads, understand?"

"Yes, sir," Cribb and Mossmuss piped in unison.

"She's turned and is headed the other way!" said Dare. "Go get her!"

Cribb and Mossmuss took off through the forest, Dare stumbling, cursing behind.

Despite her head start, Hyun-ju Sun was no match for Cribb and Mossmuss. The quick-footed Cribb caught up with her first, hooked an arm around her, and brought her down into the snow. She struggled out of Cribb's grasp, but Mossmuss puffed up, heaving angrily, and wrapped an enormous arm around her, cinching her up like a sack of flour. "Put me down!" she screamed, her legs flailing helplessly behind her.

"Nothing doing," said Mossmuss. "You've been summoned."

Mossmuss hoisted Chul's mother back to Dare, who had given up the chase and was puffing into his hands, trying to stay warm. "Put her down," said Dare, and Mossmuss plopped her unceremoniously into the snow.

Dare stood over Chul's mother. "Do you suppose that I would have been fooled? Anita Aminou and Chul Sun steal the *khar chuluu*, flee from Algiers to the Two-Hearted Forest, and the next thing I know, I find Sun Hyun-ju taking a Sunday stroll through the middle of nowhere? How stupid do you think I am? Cribb, find the *khar chuluu*."

Cribb scanned Hyun-ju for the black stone and, finding nothing, patted her down. "It ain't on her."

"What? Where is it then?"

"Where is what?" said the woman. "I don't know what you're talking about."

"Are you going to tell me that you've escaped?"

"I...we did," she said. "We split up and went different directions. I only hope that Yong-jin has found help by now."

"That is a pathetic lie, *Anita Aminou*," said Dare. He pulled out a hand-held moleculizer from his coat pocket, one of his own inventions. "I should scatter your atoms right here and now." But something made him hesitate. A flicker of doubt. There was the slightest possibility that this truly *was* Hyun-ju Sun, and if so and he killed her, then he would put his entire plan at risk. Dare shoved the moleculizer back into his pocket. "Mossmuss, pick her up. We'll take her back to the lake and get to the bottom of this. And Cribb — if you see any of the Aminous, I want you to shoot on sight. Understood?"

"Crystal clear," said Cribb, pulling out his own moleculizer.

Mossmuss hoisted Hyun-ju under his arm and they made their way back to the helicopter.

Airborne again, the helicopter mounted a crest of trees and was soon hovering unsteadily over an ice-covered pond. Anita, still in the shape of Chul's mother, clung to the seat as Mossmuss whipped the tail around as Cribb on the gun mount scanned the forest. "I don't see no one down there," he said.

"OK, take us in," said Dare from the shotgun seat.

Mossmuss flipped a switch on the console and the ice at the center of the pond melted away, revealing a pool ten meters in diameter and black as the *khar chuluu* against the white rim of the snow-covered ice.

"What? Are we gonna land in the lake?" squealed Cribb.

Dare whipped around and slapped the back Cribb's head. "No questions, numbskull. Just keep a look-out."

Mossmuss brought the helicopter down toward the black hole in the ice, the rotors whisking snow in every direction. Anita looked down in horror. It seemed as if they were going to land right in the frigid water, but about ten meters above the dark pool, she could see that it was actually empty space. An X of landing lights was visible far below. The pond was holographic, the new science version of conjuring. She scanned the forest worriedly for Chul and the magic carpet. Just then, she saw a glint of teal. Chul was hovering just below the rim of the rise. Dare noticed her looking and frowned. He slapped Mossmuss. "Take us up. Up, idiot!"

Mossmuss pulled at the controls.

"What's that?" said Dare pointing toward the flicker of color.

"It's Chul!" shouted Cribb. "He's on a..."

Blimey! He's on a flyin' carpet!"

Dare seized Hyun-ju. "I knew it! So you thought you would set a little trap, following me back to the lake, did you? Well, I have a few tricks myself. Cribb! Knock out that carpet!"

Cribb flipped a switch on the side of the weapon in the open door and sent a beam of energy at the carpet, which immediately went limp. Chul tumbled into the snow and rolled down the hill toward the edge of the pond.

"Chul!" cried Anita. She tried to scramble out of the helicopter, but Dare held her down.

He grinned at her. "You can't use your own powers while you're inside of Chul's mom! Too bad you don't have the *khar chuluu*." He slapped Mossmuss on the shoulder. "Now, go get the boy!"

"Mighty djinn, help us!" cried Anita.

A voice boomed out over the pond. "Gladly."

Dare, Cribb, and Mossmuss watched in horror as I — the Djinn of All Deserts! — rolled in over the pond, a pillar of roiling desert sand. The helicopter reeled backwards as Mossmuss struggled to keep ahold of the controls. Cribb lost his grip on the weapon and the magic carpet leaped back off the snow and glided to where

Chul was struggling to his feet. He climbed back on.

I piled my wind into a vortex around the helicopter, sending the contraption into a spiral. Anita grabbed on for dear life as I tossed the helicopter onto its side, dumping the hapless Cribb out of his seat. He shrieked like a child and grabbed ahold of a landing skid, his legs kicking the air.

"Down!" screamed Dare. "Down!"

Mossmuss struggled with the stick. "It's not safe! I can't get her in."

"Just take us down, moron!"

Mossmuss heaved the stick and righted the helicopter as Cribb scrambled off of the skid and back into the cockpit.

"Let us down, Djinn of All Deserts!" shouted Anita.

So I did. I opened the vortex under the helicopter and the silly thing dropped drunkenly, disappearing into the darkness under the false lake. Mossmuss heaved the stick and leveled the chopper, bringing it down with a thud on the concrete floor. Anita blinked hard, looking through the enfeebled eyes of Chul's mom, trying to see where they were. Her eyes grew accustomed to the dim space and she saw that they were in a cylindrical hangar bay.

"Nicely done," said Dare. "Now, quick, shut the roof and reactivate the hologram. Cribb, where's Chul?"

Cribb checked the console. "I don't know. I've lost him."

Anita nodded toward the hangar bay. "There he is."

Indeed, Chul was standing beside the helicopter, his hands in his pockets, looking as casual as could be.

Dare climbed down out of the helicopter and threw his coat to the floor. "Oh! Clever, little dude," he said. "Clever indeed. Well, do you see? I have your mother here. Or no, this isn't really your mother, is it? Just an exact replica, with Anita Aminou riding along inside. So that must mean you have the *khar chuluu*. So why don't you be a good boy and give it back to me?"

"But I don't have it," said Chul, dutifully turning out his pockets.

"Right," said Dare, sounding unimpressed. "If you don't have it, who does?"

"I do," replied Anita. She pulled the black stone out of her pocket.

"What?" said Mossmuss. "We searched you. How'd you get it?"

Are you surprised as well? Then I shall explain.

In the split second between when Mossmuss brought the helicopter to a landing and when Dare spotted Chul standing on the hangar bay floor, the boy had been busily working in super speed. His first order of business had been to find the power actuators that control the pond holograph and the hangar bay doors and fry them with an electromagnetic pulse, which took about 89 milliseconds. Next, he deactivated Cribb's crew-serve weapon on the helicopter by frying the power supply to that as well, which took another 12 milliseconds. It then took 17 milliseconds each to stealthily remove the molecularizers from the pockets of Dare, Cribb, and Mossmuss and hide them in a cupboard on the other side of the hangar bay. Finally, as planned, he delivered the *khar chuluu* back to Anita by slipping it into the pocket of Hyun-ju's jacket, which took about another 33 milliseconds — all before appearing on the hangar bay floor in front of the helicopter.

And with the *khar chuluu* safely back in her possession, Anita used the incantation to return to her own shape. Both Cribb and Mossmuss shrieked in terror to witness the process of Hyun-ju Sun transforming back into Anita Aminou. She smiled brightly. "Well, wasn't that weird? Win one for the old science." And with that, she gave a nod and flung Dare telekinetically out onto the hangar bay floor.

Chul dashed off and found a length of rope in a storage closet. Returning at super speed, he spun around Dare and bound him tightly, so fast the rope seemed to magically appear around him. Cribb and Mossmuss were disposed of in similar fashion, and soon all three were bound, back to back to back, on the hangar bay floor. Anita and Chul stood above them, arms crossed. I, meanwhile, returned to the shape of a young man and joined them at their side.

"What?" said Mossmuss. "Who are you?"

"I am the Djinn of All Deserts!"

"The what of all deserts?"

"A *genie*," said Dare. "One of those silly spirits of the old science. It looks like Chul went and made lots of little friends over the past few days. Say Chul, why don't you ask the genie to grant your wish and free your parents? Ah, but he doesn't do wishes, does he? In fact, all the genie can do is blow sand around and spy on people, isn't that right?" He twisted his shoulders and laughed. "Pathetic is what it is: Two pre-teens and a sand sprite thinking they could defeat *me*, the great-grandson of Kelnick Dare."

"We have, haven't we?" said Anita. "You're the one who's tied up on the floor, not us. Now why don't you tell us where Chul's parents are."

"Oh, they're very close, *very* close indeed. In fact, they are just beneath where you're standing right now. And well protected, I assure you, for you can't plinch down there. Your genie can't save them either. Not even Chul's electromagnetic pulse can defeat my defenses. In fact, I knew that the little magneto-genetically modified ingrate freak could cause me trouble at some point." Dare sniffed noisily. "So I put in place a purely mechanical failsafe. Would you like me to explain?"

Anita glanced nervously at Chul. "Go ahead."

"Well, you see, the pond above you is only partially holographic. All around us is forty million liters of freezing cold water. That door above us has not shut yet—so I'm guessing that

Chul disabled it with his electromagnetic pulse. What he didn't know when he was doing his thing is that the door is connected to a mechanical timer such that if it remains open for more than ten minutes, four spring-loaded sluices—one on each side of us—are activated so that ice-cold water is released into the rooms down below where we are sitting—the very rooms where Chul's lovely parents are, right now, eating their lunch, completely oblivious to what is going on above them. So what is it, Mossmuss? About six minutes since you opened the door? Maybe more, maybe six and a half? Let's call it seven, to be conservative. That would give you two very clever, very brave children—oh, and your magic genie—three minutes to figure out how to either (a) disable the mechanism or (b) find a way down there and free them. And for us, well, we get the pleasure of sitting here safe and sound and watching you figure out how to do it."

Anita turned to Chul. "Is he lying?"

"I don't know, but we can't take the chance."

Dare laughed. "Yes, don't we just love guessing games! And, no, you shouldn't take any chances with the lives of Chul's mommy and daddy. And Chul Sun, little dude, you know that

I know your powers better than you do. Do you think I would allow you to use your speed against me? Consider this: Each of the four mechanical sluices is locked behind a six-inch-thick steel vault door, each protected with not one, but two, old-fashioned, four-number combination spin locks. You can slow down time to your heart's delight, but you'll never be able to try every possible combo on all eight locks in three minutes. So it appears that you are at an impasse. Unless, that is, you would like to give up on this stupidity, release us, and allow me to disable the mechanical mechanisms."

"Oh, I think there's a simpler solution," said Anita. "I believe you've heard of the Gordian Knot? Have you, Chul?"

"No, it isn't something Dare taught me."

"Dare knows the story," said Anita. "Alexander the Great, on his march through Asia, came to a city called Gordium. In Gordium, there was a cart that had been owned by the founder of the city. The yoke of the cart was tied to a pole by a complicated and, it was said, unsolvable knot. According to legend, whoever could untie it would rule all of Asia. Alexander took one look at it, pulled out his sword, and cut the knot in half."

"A silly fairy tale, like the old science," said Dare with a smile. "You have two minutes."

"We'll see if the old science is silly or not," said Anita. She fell to her knees and, removing a marker from her pocket, drew on the floor a perfect circle, and inside the circle, she drew two triangles to form a hexagon, each of the points touching the edge of the circle. As she drew, she murmured, "By the Seven Kings I call thee. By Al-Mudhib, I call thee. By Murrah, I call thee. By Al-Ahmar, I call thee…"

Cribb, who was facing away from Anita, cocked his head and tried to see. "What's she doin'?"

"Some idiocy," grunted Dare. "Some desert chant."

Just then, Mossmuss began to panic. "Wha — what's happening?"

The ground beneath them was turning to sand and the sand was turning to liquid. Cribb, Mossmuss, and Dare began to sink. Dare screeched, "What are you doing, you crazy girl?"

Anita glanced up from her incantation. She too was sinking through the floor. So was I, the Djinn of All Deserts, and also Chul, who was looking around confusedly and with mounting alarm. "Anita, are you sure about this?"

She paid no attention, just continued the incantation until, all at once, everyone fell through the floor and crashed down into the room below in a cloud of sand and dust. Dare, Cribb, and Mossmuss, still firmly bound together, landed smack dab at the center of the table where Hyun-ju Sun and her husband Yong-jin Sun were, indeed, eating their lunch. They jumped back from the table. Anita and Chul landed behind them on a couch. I settled down lightly at their side. Above us, the ceiling had closed up and was, again, solid steel.

"What's going on?" cried Hyun-ju. "What? Chul? Is that you?"

Father, mother, and son rushed into each other's arms. "I can't believe it. Is this really you?" asked Chul's father. He appeared just as Chul had seen him in the cabin, stooped and weakened from imprisonment, but wonderfully alive. "But how? How did you get here? What happened?" He pointed at Dare, Cribb, and Mossmuss tied up on the table. "Did *you* do that?"

Chul smiled shyly. "Yes…well…but we have

no time to talk. We have to get you out of here."

"Or rather," said Anita, "Thorium Dare has to tell us how to get out of here." She kept her eyes fixed on him. "You see, the solution to your problem, Dare, is that *you* have to solve the problem. By your count we have less than two minutes. So what will you do?"

Dare was really in a state now. He struggled frantically in the ropes. "You crazy girl! There is no way! The sluices will open! And we're trapped down here!"

"Come now," said Anita, "do you mean you didn't design a way out of this room?"

"Not from the inside! Look, the only way out is through the doors behind you. They can't be opened from the inside. That's why it's called a *prison*! The controls are on the other side of the doors!"

"Maybe I can blow the doors open with an electromagnetic pulse," said Chul.

"It won't work," said Dare. "I told you, this whole place is pulse protected!"

"What about you, Djinn of All Deserts?" asked Chul. "Can you get us out?"

"I am afraid he's right," said I. "I can neither open the doors nor stop the water from coming down here."

"But," said Anita, "do you mean we're trapped down here for real?"

"Precisely, you stupid, reckless, crazy girl!"

Cribb leaned over to Mossmuss. "How much time did he say before them sluices start opening?"

"Two minutes? One minute now?" said Mossmuss.

"Probably less," croaked Dare.

"Djinn of All Deserts," said Anita, "go find my parents and bring them here right away."

"But I cannot leave you, Anita the Brave," said I.

"Anita the Crazy, more like it," said Dare. "Your parents can't save you now. This room is protected from their pathetic magic!"

"Just go," said Anita. "Tell them to come quick!" And with that I became like a coil of desert heat and disappeared into the ceiling above them.

Everyone fell silent and waited. They listened. Ten excruciating seconds went by. Another ten. Then another ten. Then they heard, one after another, a series of four faint thuds far above them followed by a muted onrush of water that grew louder and more urgent as it descended toward them. Moments later, at the four corners of the room, panels burst open and water crashed down from above. The room was filled immediately with the dank and frigid odor of icy lake water. Anita, Chul, and Chul's parents leaped up onto the couch. Cribb and Mossmuss babbled and screeched in terror.

Using her telekinetic powers, Anita tried to move a table in front of one of the holes through which the water was crashing, but the force was too strong and the table just blew away.

Chul looked at his parents. "What do we do?"

"I don't know," said his mother.

The water crashed and gurgled. Soon the floor was covered. The water rose rapidly in the room. "We need to get higher," said Chul.

Anita turned her attention to the objects around them. One by one, using her telekinetic powers, she began to stack the furniture up. She toppled the refrigerator and let it fill up with water. On the refrigerator, she stacked the washing machine and, onto these, she floated the couch where she, Chul, and Chul's parents were seated, so that their heads were just inches from the ceiling.

"What about us?" squeaked Cribb. He, Mossmuss, and Dare were still on the table, the top of which was, by now, just inches from the rising water. The room was freezing cold, chilled by the torrent. "We're going to die, mates," croaked Cribb. "This's really it." Mossmuss just blubbered like a massive baby.

"Shut up!" barked Dare. He looked up at Anita. "Move us up, will you, girl? Or are you going to watch us drown?"

After a moment of hesitation, she floated the table upon which they were seated to the other side of the room and set it on top of the bed. "Nicely done," grinned Dare. "Now we all get to watch each other drown. This will give a little last pleasure before we shuffle off our mortal coils."

Chul turned to his father. Throughout, the man had remained calm and seemed to be lost in thought. Though much reduced physically from his imprisonment, he seemed to have lost none of his mental sharpness. At last, he turned to his son and spoke in a low voice so that Dare and his men could not hear. "There is a way out."

"How?" Chul whispered.

"Through the sluices," said his father.

Chul nodded. "I thought of that, but it's too far

to swim up and the water pressure coming down is too strong."

"In super speed you would have enough time."

"Yes, but in super speed, I can't break the surface tension. Water is like concrete."

"That is why you have to move in air, not water."

"But how? I don't understand."

"Years ago, before I defected, Chul...many years ago, I studied submarine-launched ballistic missiles. A missile can't fly through water, right? So the Americans and Russians figured out how to launch the missiles out of a submarine in a bubble of air. Don't you see? It's simple. You create a bubble of air inside the pipe and you go up in the bubble. You can escape as quickly as the bubble rises up in the pipe, which should only take a few seconds."

"But how do I make a bubble?"

"I think you can guess. Wait for the room to fill up. The pressure will equalize between the room and the pipe. You won't be able to go at super speed through the water. Just move fast enough to get to the opening of the pipe. Once inside the pipe, use your EMP to vaporize the water. The gas created will create a bubble around you. The bubble will rise up through the pipe. Just go up with the bubble to the surface. Once you're in the open air, you can switch into super speed, find your way to the control room, and open the doors."

"But you all will be underwater," said Chul.

"Yes," said his father, "but if you succeed, we will only be under for a few seconds, you see?"

"And what if I don't succeed?"

"Then I am happy deep in my heart to have seen you again. And I want you to know how proud we are of you, and how very sorry for everything we have done and how you have had to suffer for our pride and ambition."

"It's not your fault," said Chul. "It's Dare's. He's the one that did this to us."

"Yes, but if we hadn't made you the way you are…"

"If you hadn't made me the way I am then I wouldn't be able to save us," said Chul. He smiled. "And if I can't, well…then I can't. I am just glad to be able to be with you one last time."

"We love you, Chul," said his mother.

"More than anything," said his father.

"I know," said Chul. And he did. Because of

the power of the *khar chuluu* to transform Anita into his mother and father, he knew they loved him, with all their hearts, minds, and souls. Chul, his father, his mother, and Anita grabbed a hold of each other as the frigid, muddy water closed in around them.

On the other side of the room, Cribb, Mossmuss, and Dare struggled up onto their knees and had their chins just above the water. Cribb was cursing terribly. Mossmuss was weeping. Dare, who had been watching Chul and his father talking in low tones, just smiled with wicked delight. "Hey, little dude and daddy!" he cried above the din of the water. "What are you two up to, eh? Plotting and scheming? Or just saying your last goodbyes? Anyway, *arrivederci*, little dude! See you on the other side!" He winked knowingly and, taking a deep breath, put his head under the water.

Chul turned away from Dare and felt the water close in over his head. In a few seconds, the crashing ended and was followed by a frigid stillness. In the murk, Chul could see the dim outlines of his parents and Anita, and beyond, a shadowy splotch that marked the mouth of one of the sluices where the water had come down into the room. It was now or never. He switched into super speed. Immediately, the cold was gone, but he felt as if he were trapped in molasses, the water was so thick around him. He backed off from super speed until he could move freely, swimming through the viscous cold, and made his way to the opening.

Reaching up into it, he found that it led to a pipe not much wider than his shoulders. By wriggling his body, he could swim up, albeit awkwardly, into the pipe. Once inside, he closed his eyes, released the inner regulator that controlled his electromagnetic power, and felt a pulse of energy leap from the surface of his skin. Just as his father said it would, the pulse turned the water all around him to vapor. Chul kicked into super speed and found himself inside a bubble the diameter of the pipe. In super speed, his feet stood on the hard surface of the water below him like the floor of an elevator and he could feel the top of the bubble above his head. He slowly backed off of super speed again until he could feel the bubble rising up inside the pipe. There was little oxygen in the heated bubble, it turned out, so he had to hold his breath. This was something his father had neglected to mention. It was dark, too—pitch black to be exact—and the journey up through the pipe seemed endless. Finally, he saw the dimmest light above him. It grew brighter and brighter until, finally, he could see out into the lake above. The bubble broke free of the pipe and it was as if he had burst into another world. The lake bottom was etched brightly under the midday sunlight pouring lucidly through the ice above. The bubble rose and hit the ice. Chul balled his fist and punched a hole in the solid sheet and burst out into the cold, bracing air above. With an exhilarating breath, he launched into super speed and, in an instant, was dry again and refreshed.

Still in super speed, Chul saw a peculiar sight. It was Georges and Maryann Aminou and me— the Djinn of All Deserts—standing by the rim of the hole above the hangar bay, looking down in. To Chul, it was as if we were statues: Georges was pointing down, his eyes wide, a frantic expression occupying his face. Maryann stood next to him, her hand over her mouth, and I, in the form of a young man, standing nearby. Chul read our expressions in an instant: We knew the others were trapped below but were uncertain how to save them.

Chul had to act fast. There was no time to be misunderstood. He came up beside us and dropped out of super speed. Georges and Maryann gasped to see him appear suddenly before them.

"No time to explain," said Chul rapidly. "I am going to go find and deactivate the defenses. Plinch down to me and as soon as you can!"

"But—" said Maryann, but Chul jumped back into super speed. He didn't hear the rest of what she said. There was no more time to talk.

In the open air and unencumbered by the lake water, he made his way down into the prison control room in a flash. He dashed around the room and inspected every control until he had found and manually deactivated all of the defenses against the old science that Dare had put into place to protect the prison. Next, he found and switched the control that opened the doors to the prison room. He dropped back into normal speed. The doors slid open, followed by a torrent of water. With Dare's defenses deactivated, Georges and Maryann detected Chul's location and plinched down immediately. Now they were standing beside Chul, their feet already submerged. He turned to them. "We have to stop more water from coming in!"

Georges took in the situation in a moment. He waded forward to the doorway, raised a hand, and sent beams of blue-white energy into the four corners of the room, sealing the sluices, preventing any more water from coming down. High up on the couch, Chul's parents and Anita gasped and shivered. They were cold and frightened, but otherwise unharmed. Chul, Georges, and Maryann struggled toward them through the draining water and lifted them down, one by one, from the soaking couch. Chul and Anita embraced their parents.

I, the Djinn of All Deserts, was there too. I took the form of a warm desert breeze and slowly warmed and dried the soaked and shivering group.

"Ha!" came a shout of delight from the other side of the room. It was Thorium Dare, looking pale and ragged—a cold, wet rat with an ingenious smile etching his crooked face. He was still tied up with Cribb and Mossmuss on the table where they spat and gagged out the dank lake water. "Well done, Chul Sun!" said Dare. "You've saved the day! And saved *me* too! I knew you'd come through in the end. No doubt about it, little dude, you have been well trained, very well trained! Say, genie, come over here and warm us up too. I'm frickin' freezing."

Needless to say, I, the Djinn of All Deserts, took no heed.

Anita turned to her mother and nodded to where Dare was prattling away. "Is there something you can do about him, Mom?"

Maryann winked at her daughter and, with a nod, put a tongue-binding spell on the troublesome great-grandson of the infamous Kelnick Dare. He immediately fell silent and stayed that way until the police came to take him to jail.

Chapter the Last

In which Chul Sun returns something stolen and Anita the Reckless faces the judgment of her stone ancestors.

H igh above the Baltic Sea, Chul Sun made his way up a set of steep and winding stone stairs carved into a hillside and worn smooth under six centuries of footsteps. At the top of this hill, perched above the crashing, frigid sea, stood an ancient and lonely castle. He had been here a week before, but so much had happened since then that it seemed like a lifetime had passed since he had pretended to be a delivery boy. He was then an orphan and a slave to Thorium Dare, sent on a mission that he knew was wrong. Now, he returned to the castle freed from Dare and reunited with his two loving parents, both of whom were alive, although weakened by six years of imprisonment. They were standing at the foot of the stairs in the parking area, arm in arm, smiling up at him. He turned every now and then, just to make sure they were still there, still really truly alive and well. He was worried that, somehow, if he did not turn to look, they might disappear. But they were always there when he turned, only growing smaller as he climbed higher toward the doors of the ancient castle.

When he arrived at the castle, instead of knocking on the deliveries door like he had before, he walked around to the front, to where a set of tall and worn wooden doors faced the battered, pewter-colored sea. Chul pulled the bell rope and waited while the salty wind buffeted his face. After some time, the great wooden doors swung open and out of the darkness inside appeared the small and gentle face of Kristjan Tormis.

The old man showed no anger toward Chul, just the touched expression of a grandfather who is surprised—and happy—to see a grandchild appear unannounced at the door. "Hello. Hello," the old man said in Estonian, which Chul understood perfectly well. "Please, come in."

He stepped into the castle and shivered. They were standing in the stone foyer of the house, lit from high windows by the calm, white light of the Baltic winter. Somehow, it seemed colder inside than outside, but Chul was warmed by the old man's gentleness and hospitality. "I have something that belongs to you," said Chul. He pulled the smooth, black stone out of his pocket. "I should not have taken this. It was wrong."

"Yes," said the old man, "it was wrong of you to take this. I trust you have learned by now what this thing can do."

"Yes," said Chul, "I'm sorry for what I've done. There are lots of things I'm sorry for."

"Oh, well, yes," said the old man. By his expression, Chul sensed that Tormis already knew much of what had transpired over the last few days, but he seemed less interested in Chul's adventures than the stone itself. He looked at it, turning it over in his hand. "It is a dark magic, is it not? The *khar chuluu*?"

"It led me back to my parents," said Chul. "It helped me find them."

Tormis nodded. "You see, the man who made

the *khar chuluu*, Eno Timur, he was not a wicked man. Ambitious, yes. Reckless, yes. Short-sighted. But we all are sometimes. And he paid the highest price for his ambition. Murdered with his wife on the threshold of his own home. A terrible tragedy. But it is said that God has not made anything — be it animal, vegetable, or mineral — that has not some light in it."

"Do you think even Dare has some light in him?" asked Chul.

Tormis shrugged. "This must be so. Maybe it is a light only the angels can see. For it is also said that wickedness comes from turning away from one's own goodness, not from destroying it. Do you see? A week ago, you were a young boy being used by a wicked man. Now, you have come here to return what belongs to my family. And for that I am grateful."

"I *am* sorry," said Chul.

"Yes, I know, and I forgive you. You have shown your light. Now go grow that light, cultivate it, like a flower. That is the best penance you can offer me or anyone else."

"Thank you, Mr. Tormis."

The old man put a thin, dry hand on Chul's shoulder. It was not cold, as he had expected, but brightly warm, like a hearthstone. "Now go back to your parents. They are waiting for you and you have much catching up to do."

Eight hours later, Chul Sun was standing in the grand, round library in the hidden desert home of the Aminou family. At the center of the room stood Anita, her eyes downcast, under the scornful gaze of her stone ancestors in their niches. At her side stood her parents, Georges and Maryann. There too was the ancient tree woman, Anita's *Jeddah*, who had been rolled into the room in a large ceramic pot. Chul and his parents stood respectfully off to the side, having been admitted in order to give testimony. As was I, the Djinn of All Deserts, where I floated at Anita's heel, a fillip of desert heat, a flicker of smokeless flame, hanging as near as possible to Anita the Reckless, Anita the Brave.

A court of judgment had been called in the Aminou library, in the ancient manner, where the practitioners of the old science were judged by their elders for the use and misuse of the old science. This evening, Anita was being judged. The girl was in trouble, to say the least. She stood accused of disobeying her parents, running away from home, binding a djinn, using the *khar chuluu* in violation of the Tripoli Conclave of 1719, and just generally having nearly gotten herself, Chul, and Chul's parents killed in the Two-Hearted Forest.

She drew a nervous figure eight on the stone floor with the toe of her shoe as she listened to her stone elders weigh in on her punishment.

"Stripped of her magic," groused Epicius the Elder from his niche. "That is what she should be. Once again, she disobeyed her parents by running away!"

"I've always said that the girl lacks proper discipline," said Gowa the Priestess. "She used forbidden magic not once but twice! She bound a dangerous djinn and used the *khar chuluu*. She led herself and others into danger!"

"A lazy girl, trying to take shortcuts to greatness!" said Ahmed the Awe Inspiring. "Using dark magic to get her way."

"Bah! Stone-faced fools!" barked the little tree woman from her pot. "This young girl accomplished what we had not been able to do in six years of trying—she found Chul Sun's parents! You heard what she said. She and that boy tricked and captured Dare's henchmen,

Cribb and Mossmuss. She sent that 'dangerous' djinn, as you call him, to her parents and so they could find Dare's secret prison in the Two-Hearted Forest. Yes, she led others into danger, but that is what leaders do."

"She got lucky, and you know it," said the Iroquois clan mother. "She went out seeking her fortune, not what was right. This is the problem."

"True," said Anita's *Jeddah*. "But who among us did not go out seeking our fame when we were young? Who among us did not want to win the approval and admiration of our parents and our ancestors—to be thought of as a great witch or wizard, chief or chieftess? Have you considered that she took all of those risks to prove herself to you fools? So she could join your ranks? Look before you. Use your eyes, though they are made of stone! Thorium Dare—the last in that wicked family line—is in prison. Chul Sun and his parents have been reunited. The three *khar chuluu* have been returned to each of their rightful owners. Yet you all demand that she be punished!"

With this, the stone figures fell silent in their niches. They cast their eyes away from Anita in bitterness and shame.

"In any case, it is us," said Maryann, "who will decide what punishment is appropriate for our daughter. But first, we think Anita should be allowed to speak in her own defense."

Anita, whose eyes had remained on her feet during this whole proceeding, lifted them and looked at the figures in the niches. She looked at her *Jeddah* in her pot. At Chul Sun and his parents. At her own parents.

"My ancestors are right. I enslaved this djinn and went to Algiers with the *khar chuluu* because I thought I could find Thorium Dare and defeat him by myself. I took all of my savings to Mo Kateb, hoping that he would tell me the secret of the *khar chuluu* because I thought it would somehow allow me to beat Dare. All this is true.

"The truth is also that I could not defeat Thorium Dare. Even after seeing Mo Kateb use the *khar chuluu*, it was Chul who had to show me how to use it. I could not have captured Cribb and Mossmuss without the help of Chul and the Djinn of All Deserts. I could not have found Dare's secret prison, either, without them. And there is no way I could have defeated Dare and saved Chul's parents without Chul and the djinn and Chul's parents and my parents.

"My *Jeddah* is kind to say that I am a leader. But leaders listen to others and rely on others. They don't run off and think they can do everything by themselves. So, yes, my ancestors are right. I did wrong. I ran away to do something alone that I could not do. I put others in danger, and I am sorry. And for this, I put myself at your mercy."

Maryann said, "And so—"

"May I speak?" This voice came from me, the Djinn of All Deserts. Everyone looked up in surprise. I had taken my new favored form, that of a young man in a simple robe, and stood before them, humble, hoping to make myself heard.

"It is unusual," said Georges, "for a djinn to interfere in human affairs."

"Yes, it is," said I. "It is quite unusual. But this is an unusual young girl. In any case, I do not mean to interfere, only to speak my heart."

"Speak then."

"I have lived in this desert for five thousand years and for five thousand years have lived as a slave to men and women. Some have been wicked. Some have been good. Most have been blinded by their greed or ambition or small human concerns. They had many desires and they tried to use my powers to get the things that they wanted — wealth, power, immortality. None of them has succeeded. They have all returned to dust. Their power and ambitions died with them. Their wealth scattered and gone.

"But none of these men and women, until this young girl, has ever sought my counsel. None has ever asked me for my advice. This is no small thing for a djinn. For, you see, I am not here because Anita the Brave has bound me. She did not know — maybe it was an oversight in her magical training — that when a human asks a djinn for guidance, the djinn is no longer bound. The slave can never guide the master. You see? I stand here, unbound, and have been so since the moment she sought my counsel in the Two-Hearted Forest. I am here as a friend to Anita Aminou. I speak not as a slave, but as a being who has seen a glimmer of greatness in this young girl. I must soon return to the desert from which I came. But before I depart, I wanted to say this. Punish this girl if you must, for that is yours to decide, but know that she has earned *this* djinn's admiration."

Maryann glanced up at Anita's ancestors, a twinkle in her eyes. "Well, I believe we have all said our peace on the matter of Anita Aminou.

And as for your punishment, Anita, it shall be as prescribed. The minimum we are allowed by family law and in consideration for all the good that our daughter has done."

Georges put his hand on Anita's shoulder. "Two months grounding and six months without magical powers."

Her shoulders shrank, half with relief that her punishment had not been harsher, half with disappointment that it was as harsh as it was.

"Half a year as a helpless human," said her *Jeddah*. "Ouch."

"School in America will be starting back up again soon," said Maryann. "Anita will come back with us to Atlanta. She will get the chance to learn what it is like to be a normal girl. To learn to appreciate her powers."

"And what about Chul?" asked Anita.

"I'll be going back to Palo Alto with my parents," he said.

"But we'll come to see you at spring break," said Chul's mom. "We will see each other again, we promise."

"And as for me," said I, "I will be where I have lived for millennia, under the sands around you. And when you become old enough to use the Seal of Sulayman without being punished, come and see me."

"That's a long time," said Anita sadly.

"It is years, but it is also just a moment. You will see." I bowed to Anita the Kind, Anita the Brave, then turned and bowed to the others in the grand old library. "Until then, goodbye, Anita. Goodbye, everyone."

And with a genteel flourish, I, the Djinn of All Deserts, drew myself up into a whirlwind of dust and warmth that spread out with spectral fingers and disappeared into the walls of the ancient library of the Aminou ancestral home.

The statues in their niches returned to their stone postures, and Maryann took Anita by the hand and smiled. The time of judgment was over. The dinner bell rang and the Aminou and the Sun families followed the warm smell of lamb and saffron rice to the dining hall where they sat down to a long and happy dinner under a vault of desert stars.

ACKNOWLEDGMENTS

Thanks to Ella, whose wonderful imagination was the creative spark for this story. Thanks to Christopher Noël for his expert editing and encouragement during the writing process. Thanks to the staff and students of the New York Writers Workshop for their insights and advice. Most everything I know about djinn came from *Legends of the Fire Spirits: Jinn and Genies from Arabia to Zanzibar* by Robert Lebling. All imaginative departures are mine. Thanks to Kenneth Grahame, A. A. Milne, Rudyard Kipling, and all of the masters of the old science that inspired the style of this book. And thanks to my family. I love you always.

For more information on the
author visit www.wilsonwhitlow.com.